NO TIME TO TALK

There was a kid behind them in the stand with a pair of field glasses. Neely jerked the glasses out of his hand.

"What the hell's going on?" T.Z. asked.

"I already told you," Neely said, as if to a child. "Shut up."

Then he yanked the glasses from his eyes and plumped them back in the kid's lap. He started walking very fast for the exit from the ballpark.

T.Z. had to half run to keep up. "What's wrong, Neely?"

But Neely didn't say anything more than "Just keep your head down and move as fast as you can."

T.Z. always got scared. He was scared now. "What's wrong, Neely? Tell me, please. What's wrong?"

"Like I said," Neely said through gritted teeth, "keep your head down and move as fast as you can."

That was when Neely broke into a full run and headed for the maze of the railroad yard down in the valley below.

T.Z., trying to keep up, said, "I'm scared, Neely. I'm really scared."

But all Neely could think about was the glimpse of the fat man in the bleachers and who the man was. And why he'd be here.

ED GORMAN

GRAVES' RETREAT

LEISURE BOOKS   NEW YORK CITY

A LEISURE BOOK®

December 1999

Published by

Dorchester Publishing Co., Inc.
276 Fifth Avenue
New York, NY 10001

ISBN 0-8439-4655-5

*This is for the Driscoll family,
and especially for my mother Bernadine,
with love.*

ACKNOWLEDGMENTS

Cedar Rapids has been blessed with many fine historians whose works I've drawn upon as background. Here I would like to acknowledge my debt to:

Ralph Clements, *Tales of the Town* (Stamats Publishing, 1967)

Ernie Danek, *Tall Corn and High Technology* (Windsor Publications, 1980)

Harold F. Ewoldt and his many fine historical pieces in the Cedar Rapids *Gazette*

Janette Stevenson Murray and Frederick Gray Murrary, *The Story of Cedar Rapids* (Stratford House, 1950)

The Cedar Rapids *Gazette* archives and Dale Kueter's piece on the Fourth in particular

Not least I would like to thank my editor, Gerald Gladney, for his belief in this project.

While most of the history contained herein is accurate, certain liberties have been taken for dramatic purposes.
—Ed Gorman

The sacrifice acceptable to God is a broken spirit; a broken and contrite heart, O God, thou wilt not despise.

PSALM 51:17

GRAVES' RETREAT

CHAPTER ONE

On the morning of April 26, 1884, in Piedmont, Missouri, a Roman Catholic priest with a curiously angry blue gaze stood on the depot platform as the baggagemaster began loading up the train car for the trip west.

The priest stood next to a steamer trunk that was tall enough to touch his elbow. It was metal and black and battered and when the baggagemaster got a dolly under it, he glanced up at the priest and said, "You pack your parish in here, Father?" Obviously, he hoped the cleric would find humor in his remark.

The priest smiled. All except for his blue eyes. "I'm going to an Indian reservation in Iowa. I plan to be there several years. Everything I own is in that trunk."

The baggagemaster laughed. "The way this trunk handles, Father, you could be on that reservation for several *decades*, let alone years."

The priest wore thick, steel-rimmed eyeglasses. He brushed some dandruff from the shoulder of his black cassock and said, "God will bless you for helping me."

With that, the priest strode down the platform, carrying a somber gray carpetbag, to the six passenger cars. On his way he passed a typical assortment of depot people—society ladies in big, flowered hats (though it was only April, the temperature had already hit 62, and apple blossoms kissed the breeze); businessmen glancing importantly at their pocket watches as if the universe ran on their time schedules; and various Indians, Mexicans and melting pot immigrants who looked dirty, sullen and always at least a little bit frightened. Flowered hats and pocket watches pulled out like weapons could be imposing if you were only three months away from Poland and spoke scarce English.

The priest handed the conductor his ticket, then boarded one of the cars.

Aboard, he found a window seat. The priest watched the scenery

roll by, rivers becoming plains and plains becoming hills and hills
becoming forests and forests becoming farms with black-and-white
dairy cows looking snug as they lay lazy on green grass on the shade
side of oaks and elms, or next to the gaunt shapes of Halladay Standard windmills. (The priest had even thought to himself occasionally
how nice it would be to be a cow: no human grief to make you weary,
and no fear of death because death itself was not a concept to you).

The priest settled immediately and irresistibly into staring out at
the countryside. The anger had not left his blue gaze.

Morning became afternoon. At one point he saw a ragged group of
Indians walking parallel to the tracks. Presumably they were headed
to a reservation. The Indian wars were coming to an end. The slaugh-
ter was such that white men were being paid two dollars for each
Indian corpse they buried. But not just white men. The whites were
no more innately evil than Indians, some of whom hunted and killed
their own kind for the same amount of money.

Afternoon became night. From his carpetbag the priest took a slice
of chicken, and a bottle of water. He ate quickly and without pleasure.

He watched moon-up as the silver ball was first only a vague circle
against the red-streaked dusk sky but then became more and more
vivid. He had reverence for the moon—he had read somewhere how
the Aztecs used to stand naked on nights of full moon and let its rays
fill them and give them courage for their bloody duties—and the
image had never left him.

He opened the window. The train was passing a half-mile stretch of
forest. A piney perfume almost made the priest swoon. He closed his
eyes and dozed until a conductor came up and announced, "Next
stop Grinnell! Next stop Grinnell!"

Then the priest came fully awake and sat up straight.

The time was here.

At last.

The time he always feared.

The time he always returned to again and again.

The stop at Grinnell was scheduled to be fifteen minutes but in fact
it took nearly half an hour.

The priest stood on the platform, enjoying the smell of new grass from the nearby prairie, and the sight of fireflies flickering in the darkness.

Then he was back on the train and he could feel the rail joints below him ticking off the miles of the train's inevitable progress.

It was when the next stop was announced that the priest began to perspire unduly.

By the time the train pulled into the small Iowa town, the priest was soaked.

Quickly, he yanked his carpetbag from the seat next to him and hurried out of the car.

"Good night, Father," the conductor said.

The priest gulped, seeming unable to find his voice. "Good night."

The priest went down the platform to the baggage car. The night smelled of train oil and grease and coal.

This was the part that needed to go precisely.

In fact, T.Z. should already be standing on the platform by now, and they should be leaving.

But T.Z. was nowhere in sight.

The stooped man from the depot here banged on the baggage car. "Hey, open up in there!"

All the priest could do was watch, his heart wanting to tear through his chest.

"Hey!" the depot man yelled again, banging once more. To a passenger, he said, "Some of these young bucks, they bring along a little whiskey with 'em sometimes and fall asleep."

But the priest knew better than that.

The priest knew that something was wrong.

He moved quickly, getting back on board, rushing down the corridor so he could come to the baggage car from an angle the baggage-master could not see.

He pushed down the narrow corridor till he came to the door of the baggage car.

Unlike the depot man, when the priest knocked, it was discreet. And furtive.

"T.Z.? T.Z.? Open up in there!" the priest said, knowing he could afford little more than a whisper.

But there was no response.

By now the depot man was banging again. And hollering.

The priest knew that he had only seconds, if that.

"T.Z.! T.Z.!"

The door opened and there stood T.Z.

The steamer trunk he'd been inside was wide apart and empty. That was the first fact that imposed itself on the priest's mind. The second was that the blue and white bandanna was on the floor. T.Z.'s face was open for anyone to see. The agreement was that T.Z. would always wear his mask, just as the priest would always wear eyeglasses (the Roman collar was a disguise; people noticed little else). They had perpetrated nineteen robberies and never once before had their faces been seen.

In one hand T.Z. held a black satchel. In the other he held his arm. He had been stabbed. In the flickering shadows of the kerosene lamp, his shirt sleeve was a dark red color.

Then the priest looked beyond T.Z. to the guard who rode in the baggage car. Somehow T.Z., despite the fact that he'd been stabbed, had managed to bind and gag the man.

The priest said, "He's seen us, T.Z. He's seen us. He can identify us."

"What are we going to do?" T.Z. said hysterically.

From outside the banging continued.

"We have to stay calm, T.Z. Calm." From the hard anger in his eyes, it was hard to say whom the priest hated more, the baggageman or his partner.

"I don't want a price on my head."

"Neither do I, T.Z."

"But he's seen us!"

The priest smiled. "No, T.Z., he's seen *you*."

The priest looked around at the car. At first he saw nothing that would help him. Then he found the crowbar. He went over and picked it up. He liked the feel of the cold and unforgiving steel.

He struck the man once across to stop of the skull and then across the temple. The man was dead.

The depot man was now yelling for help.

All the priest and T.Z. had time to do was escape out the other side of the train and run down the tracks into the maze of boxcars.

As he ran, T.Z. sobbed.

CHAPTER TWO

It was not an easy game to play because the rules kept changing. It was those goddamn Easterners. If they weren't monopolizing industries, then they were altering the rules of Iowa's favorite pastime.

Four years ago for example, in 1880, you needed to get eight balls for a base on balls and the distance from the mound to home plate was forty-five feet and only sissies needed to wear straps of leather let alone gloves to catch fly balls.

But forty-eight calendar months later everything had changed completely. Now you only needed six balls for a walk and the mound was fifty feet away, and be damned if everybody wasn't wearing actual baseball mitts. About the only thing that hadn't changed was the fact that there was only one umpire—and there was even talk of changing that.

The team on the field at the moment, the Cedar Rapids municipal team it was, abided by these and all the other rules in hopes that they would someday be even a whisper as good as an Iowa farm boy every one of them idolized and envied, Captain Adrian Constantine Anson ("Cap" to his fans), a strapping blond legend who played for the Chicago White Stockings and who earned the unheard-of salary of $8,000 per annum and who was sure to play in the something called the First World Series at the end of this coming season.

It was five-thirty in the afternoon. Late June. There was a sweet-scented breeze thanks to the apple blossom trees in the city park behind the baseball stadium, which consisted of three sections of bleachers angled to resemble a triangle, so that from the center section home plate and the rest of the field extended. Nearby you could hear the water going over the dam on the First Avenue bridge, and smell the summer fish. Ten degrees hotter, the smell would have been unpleasant. But now it seemed a perfect complement to the apple blossoms.

The team at bat wore gray uniforms. *New* gray uniforms. There had been a fund drive this spring. The men lived up to their uniforms, too. They were all clean-shaven except for the fancy mustaches they sported à la baseball players back East. This was the second team and this game was only a scrimmage, which explained why the bleachers were barely one-third filled.

The team on the field wore white. This was the first team, as could be deduced from the way those in the bleachers watched, fascinated, as the pitcher on the mound went into his windup.

The pitcher's name was Graves, Les Graves. A slender man with brown hair that was starting to recede, and blue eyes that were never quite without a hint of sadness, Graves looked a bit older than his twenty-six years until the very moment of the windup, when he looked no more than eighteen. Local sportswriters said Graves had "the fastest throwing arm outside of Sterling itself." (Sterling, Illinois, had an Irishman who could throw a ball faster than most people could spit on the sidewalk.)

Graves released the ball.

The umpire seemed to cry "Strike!" even before the whirling white globe reached the plate.

And there was no doubt about the trueness of the pitch. It hurtled across the home base, little more than a white blur that dipped deviously right at the befuddled batter's knees.

"Go to it, Les!" shouted the people in the stands.

No other player on the team inspired the whistles, shouts and stamping feet Les Graves did.

"One more'n the game's over!" yelled several other people.

"Strike him out real good!"

"Give 'em your Jean Laffite!"

The "Jean Laffite" was so named by a sportswriter because he claimed that it had the "destructive force of a cannon ball hurled from the grand Frenchman's warship."

So Les gave 'em "Jean" and "Jean" caused the batter to jerk back several full inches from the plate as the umpire once again called "Strike!"

The game was over.

The team manager, a chunky bald fireman named Harding, came up and threw his arm around Les. "You keep it up, Les, you'll be playing for the New York Mets." That was the team everybody was betting on to be the best in the National League. Then he said, "Hell's bells, you get any better, Sterling's going to *have* to play us."

Les just smiled.

By sunset half an hour later, the stadium was empty. For most folks this was suppertime and mothers and wives did not abide men or boys who missed supper.

Les Graves sat in the bleachers alone. There was a tune he liked. A sad tune. He hummed it to himself.

He had a habit of throwing the ball up into the air at such an angle that he had to reach way out to grab it. He felt this helped improve him as a defensive player. He needed to have some additional skill other than his pitching because he was a terrible batter.

But he paid no attention to his little game now, doing it all unconsciously. His blue eyes watched the road that ran in back of the stadium.

The road where Susan said she'd be.

The road where, now, Susan was nowhere to be found.

He threw the ball up a few more minutes, stopping when he missed one and it cracked hard against his knee.

Then he climbed to the top bleacher where he had a pretty good look at the city, a place the mayor called, with monotonous determination, "the Chicago of Iowa." But it was a quickly growing town, no doubt about it, eighteen thousand inhabitants, the service of many different railroads, more than sixty electric lights (mostly used in hotels and businesses) and a telephone company with at least two hundred and fifty connections in the city, and connections with seventy-five cities and towns outside.

There was no doubt about it. Cedar Rapids was a good place to live. Clean, progressive, honest in its government.

His time here had been the happiest in his life until he met Susan Edmonds, daughter of the man for whom he worked. He'd had another girl here, May, but when he'd met Susan— But he sensed their relationship was at its end. A part of him just wanted her to pronounce the funeral words and get it over with. She was a banker's daughter and way out of his class—

His eyes searched every access to the stadium for sight of her.

But his heart told him a truth his eyes did not need to confirm.

She would miss their meeting (he'd written her a letter yesterday, asking her to come here now) because she was afraid to say what she really wanted to say—

To let him explain why he'd become so angry Sunday night and said the things he had.

He stood there in his white uniform till stars began to appear in the bluish haze of night sky. Dogs lonely as he bayed at the silver disc of moon. Down on First Street he could hear the player pianos and the roar of beery laughter.

He was just turning to go—wanting a beer now, wanting at least loud if not decent companionship—when below the bleachers he heard the clopping of a single horse and saw the shape of her carriage.

He felt exultant that she was here and terrified she'd only come to say good-bye.

"You got my letter?"

He could scarcely see her. Hovering in the back of her small carriage.

Hiding, really.

He decided not to pester her. Afraid she might bolt and run like a frightened doe.

"I'm glad to see you, Susan."

Still, she said nothing.

He just sensed her staring at him.

He said, "I struck out eleven batters tonight."

She said, "I need a little more time to think, Les. To know my feelings."

"All right."

"I'm trying to do what's best for both of us."

"I know."

She said, "I saw May today."

"Oh?"

"And she looked lovely. Really lovely."

"May is lovely. That doesn't mean I care about her."

She leaned forward and touched his hand gently and said, "Good night, Les."

"Good night."

He watched her carriage recede into the gloom, the lonely sound of the single horse filling the night.

CHAPTER THREE

"Morning, Les."

"Morning, George."

"Beautiful day."

"It sure is."

George, a gray-haired man who worked in the teller's station next to Les, leaned forward and whispered, "You look terrible, Les."

"Didn't sleep?"

"Drinking?"

Despite his mood, Les smiled. George was forty-eight. His last son had just left home to go to business college in Chicago. George needed a younger one to look after. Les was a natural choice. "No," Les said, "I wasn't drinking. At least not much."

"Pearly's?"

Les sighed. "That I have to admit to. Pearly's is where I drank."

George, who wore a green eyeshade and a black sleeve garter and whose fingers were permanently stained with ink, clucked. "You know the kind of trouble you can get into."

Almost to himself, Les said, "Maybe that's why I went there."

George Buss looked stricken. Then he peered closer at Les, as if he were a doctor and Les a new virus. "You—aren't still sneaking around seeing his daughter Susan, are you?"

But before Les could answer, the second of three doors on the east side of the bank opened up. A tall, trim man in an expensive blue, Edwardian-cut suit stepped out, holding well-manicured hands to either lapel of his coat. With his golden hair and confident brown gaze and almost arrogantly angled mustache, he looked like the sort of man who was always captain of the rowing team at Yale.

He proceeded then to walk down the length of the six teller stations, a military man inspecting the troops. And that's how the tellers —three men, three women—responded. Throwing their shoulders straight back. Tricking out their mouths with gleaming smiles. Nodding a by-God-and-by-gumption nod to the man.

Kind monarch that he was, the golden man nodded in return. It was best to give the troops a feeling of self-esteem. This made them willing to work longer hours and ask for fewer raises.

The golden man, who was named Byron Fuller, paused when he came to Les. "Feeling all right today, Mr Graves?"

Les nodded. "A touch of the flu."

Fuller studied him. Then he smiled. "I hope it was nothing more serious than a few stolen hours at Pearly's."

Next to Les, George Buss broke out into a sweat.

"Pearly's, Mr. Fuller?" Les said, once he'd found his voice. That was their contract. They called him "Mr." and he called them "Mr." or "Miss" or "Mrs."

The faint smile remained on Fuller's mouth. "Certainly you've heard of the place, Mr. Graves."

"Oh, I've heard of it."

"And certainly you've even visited it once or twice."

Les cleared his throat. His shoulders were still thrown back. He was still trying to smile, the way Mr. Fuller wanted them to smile seven hours a day, five days a week. "Well, once maybe."

Fuller looked at George Buss. "Now, if you were a wagering man, would you think that Mr. Graves had visited Pearly's only once during his two years in Cedar Rapids?"

George gulped. "I—I wouldn't know, sir."

Fuller smiled back at Les. "Well, between us and the lamppost, Mr Graves, I sincerely hope you did 'tie one on' last night, and I hope it was at Pearly's."

"You do, Mr. Fuller?"

"I certainly do."

"And why would that be, if you don't mind my asking?"

This time Fuller—who was behaving strangely indeed—allowed himself an outright chuckle. "Because you're going to get some news today, Mr Graves, that will make you glad you allowed yourself to celebrate last night."

Les glanced anxiously at George, then back to Fuller. "Would that be good news or bad news, Mr. Fuller?"

And with that, Fuller reached inside the teller station and slapped Les on the back as if they were the oldest and best of friends. "Why, good news for you—and great news for the whole city of Cedar Rapids!"

Then, quickly as his good mood had come up, it vanished. He made an elaborate gesture of taking his pocket watch from his vest pocket and of scrutinizing it as if for some flaw.

"It is now eight fifty-nine and forty-two seconds." He nodded formally to the bank guard, tubercular man who Fuller insisted wear enough weaponry to intimidate the entire James gang. "The door, Spencer, if you please."

Just as the door was opening, and just as Fuller started to move snappily back to his office, he turned back to Les and said, "You appear to have won yourself another admirer, Mr Graves."

"Who would that be, Mr Fuller?"

"Last night my fiancée, Susan, said she drove down and watched you pitch at scrimmage. She said you struck out eleven men."

With that he retired to his office.

Les spent the rest of the morning thinking of two things—Susan and the mysterious "news" promised by Byron Fuller.

Not that he had a great deal of time to consider either subject at length. The bank was busy. The Fourth of July was at hand.

Several times Les looked up to see Byron Fuller, hands behind his back, rocking a bit on his heels and smiling at him.

What was going on?

But just when he started to ponder the matter, another line formed in front of his station. The women were given to bonnets and flowered hats; the men to Stetsons and fedoras. At one point a few severely dressed Amish people were in his line.

Usually, while they waited, customers contented themselves with appraising the bank's interior, most of which was done in real mahogany, with flocked wallpaper and genuine marble for counters. There were also a number of Civil War paintings, of the impossibly heroic school, with soldier eyes glowing and muzzle-smoke white as the clouds of heaven itself. Many of the customers had been in the war and knew better. Young boys lying bloody and dead—be damned the color of their uniforms—looked anything but heroic.

And so the morning went.

Around eleven George Buss, whose station was quiet for the moment, leaned over and said, "It sure must be big news. Look."

And he pointed to the glass wall of Clinton Edmonds' office.

Edmonds stood with his important thumbs hooked importantly in either of his vest pockets. He stood next to Byron Fuller. Edmonds, who with his chunky but muscular body and his white mutton-chop sideburns resembled President Chester Arthur himself, was obviously staring at Les.

And, like Byron Fuller, smiling.

"It surely must be big. Real big," George Buss said. Then he adjusted his green eyeshade and black sleeve garter and got ready to greet another line of bubbly ladies and sulky men.

But however big—or small—the news might be, Edmonds and Fuller apparently planned to keep it to themselves for a time longer because as soon as Karl Halliman, the editor of the *Enquirer,* appeared, the three men repaired to the boardroom. Edmonds himself entered last (Les could see all this from the teller station) and thumbed a gummy yellow strip of paper to the doorknob, which every bank employee knew was the official symbol of DO NOT DISTURB. Nobody was permitted to use the symbol but Edmonds himself, and nobody was permitted to disturb him if it was out.

Les looked up at the clock, not knowing what to do. His lunch hour started in five minutes. Should he wait and see if they called him in or—

But he needed food.

His bout at Pearly's last night had left him weak. And there was a game tonight.

He needed food, good food, and in decent quantities. He thought of the Charter House restaurant, of the way they fixed roast beef and mashed potatoes with gravy and bright green peas.

He was making himself weak . . . he was so hungry. He was just closing and locking his cash drawer and about to leave his station when—

The boardroom door opened. Byron Fuller came out, looked around, then summoned the guard over. The man listened to what Fuller had to say, then nodded.

He disappeared quickly.

Byron stood there, obviously waiting. Once his eyes met Les'. This time Byron's smile was a positive grin.

The guard returned, carrying a silver pitcher of water cold enough to raise silver sweat on the sides.

He handed the pitcher to Byron Fuller and then both men headed back to where they'd come from.

The yellow piece of paper was still on the boardroom doorknob. Les and his appetite headed for the Charter House.

He was three steps down the block, already taking in the sweet smells of spring flowers in Greene Square, when he heard behind him someone shout, "Les! Les Graves! Come back here!"

When he turned, he saw Byron Fuller running down the bank steps toward him.

Fuller was out of breath when he reached Les. Graves had always thought of Fuller as an exceptionally stuffy man. Now he resembled an excited teenager.

"You're having lunch with us."

"Us?"

"Yes. Mr. Edmonds and Mr. Halliman and myself." He slid his arm around Les and began escorting him up the street. "This is the greatest thing that's happened to Cedar Rapids since we paved First Avenue."

And with that, Les and Byron Fuller joined a smiling Mr. Edmonds and a beaming Mr. Halliman, and the four of them set off down the street paralleling a happy load of streetcar passengers.

"This is certainly a fine day." Mr. Edmonds laughed.

In two years of working for the man, Les had never heard Mr. Edmonds laugh before.

CHAPTER FOUR

Neely woke up on the hotel room floor and immediately grabbed the Navy Colt he always kept next to him.

The scream still reverberated in his head.

Then he realized that it had only been T.Z. and one of his nightmares.

He cursed and laid his head back down against the rolled-up clothes that served him as a pillow.

The room was decent enough—double bed, recently varnished bureau, closet, polished kerosene lamp, two plump chairs for sitting —but he slept on the floor because with T.Z.'s nightmares you never got any sleep. T.Z. either woke up yelling he was suffocating or shouting, "Don't close your eyes!" T.Z.'s father had died in his arms when T.Z. was only thirteen and T.Z. had dreams about how there, right at the last, he had sobbed, "Don't close your eyes!" knowing that when he did he would be gone for eternity.

Neely propped himself up on one elbow and rolled himself a cigarette. His hangover was bad enough that he was pasty and dehydrated. He needed a bath and a shave. He despised being dirty.

From below, the sounds of noontime Cedar Rapids floated up. The chink of rig chains as wagons plied the streets; the clang of trolley car bells; a squeeze box playing a polka in the square down the street. Warm sunshine streamed in through the window, tumbling with dust molts, covering Neely in gold and making him feel lazy as a cat, something the beefy six-foot-two man was unaccustomed to. He had grown up in Kansas plowing up ground and beating out prairie fires with wet sacks and wishing to hell he could escape from it all.

He relaxed, inhaled his cigarette, tried not to think about the old days. That was T.Z.'s problem. In a very real sense, the man's life ended with his father there in his arms that cold March night.

Whereas Neely's life, or so Neely hoped, was all ahead of him, everything up to now mere prelude to a much finer and more fascinating span of years.

And Cedar Rapids, Neely thought, was going to help bring it about. If all went as planned, this would be the easiest and perhaps the most money either of them had ever made.

T.Z. started screaming again and this time Neely, with his hangover, with his whole weariness of T.Z., got up and grabbed the slender man and slapped him hard enough across the face to draw blood.

T.Z. came awake instantly, terrified.

"My father—," he started to say.

"To hell with your father," Neely said. "To hell with him."

Then he got dressed and went outside into the lovely warm day and looked for the sight of a striped barber pole. He got himself a shave and a haircut for fifteen cents, then he went back to the hotel and got himself a bath for fifty cents.

When he returned to the room, he found T.Z. lying on his back asleep. He had a rosary of brown beads tangled up in his hands.

Neely sighed and went over to wake him up. He had been taking care of T.Z. for many years now. But soon that would be over. T.Z. had become a burden. He was going to kill T.Z. He had only to figure out how and when.

"They make a sandwich out of beef tenderloin that is not to be believed," Byron Fuller said to Les Graves once they were seated in the men's club where the elite males of the city generally lunched.

Les had seen pictures of New York City and San Francisco hotels and it was difficult to imagine they could be much fancier than this. Flocked red wallpaper and long, narrow mirrors gave the eatery the aspect of a fancy lobby. A long bar, padded in leather with matching leather chairs, ran along the west wall, while to the east more than twenty large, round tables sprawled. Six hand-tooled leather chairs went with each table. The atmosphere was positively festive. Men, Les recognized as lawyers, doctors, merchants and members of what the town's eleven different newspapers referred to as "the carriage trade," sat around the tables laughing and smoking cigars and ordering drinks from young women, some of them pretty, with hair back in buns and long white aprons over gingham dresses. On the walls were large photographs of various heroes—Abraham Lincoln, President Arthur, "Cap" Constantine and (as something of a joke) a woman named Rose Coghlan who was presently going around the country and beating men (if you could believe it!) at pigeon shooting.

"So why don't you try it?"

Les turned back to Byron, realizing he hadn't heard what the man said to him.

Byron, obviously seeing that Les had been taking in the place and was duly impressed, said, "Quite a place here, isn't it, Les?"

"It sure is." For just that moment, Les sounded very young and impressionable. He saw the amused glance exchanged by Mr. Edmonds and the newspaperman Mr. Halliman.

Their serving woman came and Byron Fuller said, "Rosie, we'll have the beef tenderloin sandwich." He indicated himself and Les. He nodded to the two other men and smiled. "These two gentlemen will have to speak for themselves."

Les sat up as straight as he could, tugging his coat down, hoping his collar was clean enough (he usually wore collars three days), hoping his looking around didn't mark him as too much a rube, despite the way Mr. Edmonds and Mr. Halliman had glanced at each other.

The other two men ordered.

Then, when Rosie was gone, Mr. Edmonds took out a very fat stogie, snipped off its end, and then put it with a certain ceremonial flair between his teeth.

Mr. Halliman said, "You'll have to forgive Clinton here, Les. He likes to keep you in suspense as long as possible."

Byron Fuller chuckled. "He certainly does. The night I asked him for Susan's hand in marriage, he told me to go for a walk for an hour —alone—and then come back." He patted his stomach. "That's not good for a fellow's digestion."

Les formed an image of Susan in his mind—in the shadows of her carriage last night—sounding so unhappy.

Clinton Edmonds exhaled a mighty cloud of smoke. "What they're trying to say, Les, is that I've been working on a little project for the past four months—and that it's finally come to fruition."

Les didn't know what to say. He just sort of gulped and sort of wondered again if his collar was clean enough to be sitting in a place such as this.

Clinton Edmonds said, "What's the one baseball team you'd most like to play?"

Les said, "I guess there isn't any doubt about it, sir. Sterling. But they'd never play us. They say we aren't on their level."

Here Clinton Edmonds broke into a grin that lost him twenty years. "Well, guess who the Cedar Rapids baseball team is going to be playing right here this coming Fourth of July!"

Suddenly Les was caught up in the same exhilaration as the others. "You're not joshing?"

"Of course I'm not joshing," Clinton Edmonds said.

"The Sterling municipal team?"

"Yes, indeed, and in our home stadium."

Les forgot for the moment to whom he was speaking and blurted, "But how did you work it?"

Clinton Edmonds put down his cigar and frowned. "Well, I wish I could say that I manipulated it the way I helped manipulate the last Republican caucus." This brought a faint smile from Mr. Halliman. "But I'm afraid what happened was this: Sterling has this exhibition game all set up with a group of men who used to play in the National League, the White Stockings and teams like that. That was going to be their Fourth of July attraction, only the National Leaguers got a much better offer to do the same thing in Fort Wayne."

Edmonds' words came as no surprise to anybody at the table. Last year the Fort Wayne, Indiana, baseball club, which had always been considered very progressive, made history by playing a seven-inning night game—one illuminated by seventeen electric lights.

"So," Edmonds went on, "Sterling found itself, last week, in a very embarrassing position. They had nobody to play."

"But why would they agree to come here?"

Edmonds laughed. "I guess because they don't have anything better to do." For the first time he looked at Les with the eye of a jeweler appraising a stone. "So, Les, do you think you can beat Sterling?"

"I—"

But before he could finish, Byron clapped him on the back and said, "Of course he can beat Sterling. Les could play in the National League if he put his mind to it."

Halliman laughed. "In the East they've got an animal called a press agent. Sounds like that's the role you're playing for young Graves here, Byron."

Les averted his eyes from Byron. Given his relationship with Susan, Les wanted—perhaps even needed—to dislike his rich young rival.

But he couldn't. Stuffy though he might be, Byron Fuller was a fair and decent young man.

"What's *your* answer, Les?" Clinton Edmonds said. The humor had gone from his voice. Byron Fuller and Karl Halliman were appropriately sober.

Sterling really is his sore spot, Les thought. Around the bank it was said that Clinton Edmonds hated the city of Sterling more than he hated anything else. And he was a man of considerable anger. A certain cabal of men in the state legislature in Sterling, it was said, had conspired to pass laws that forced Edmonds to divest himself of certain small-town banking interests. His fortune, still large, was nonetheless not what it had been. Les could see that for Clinton Edmonds this would be much more than a simple baseball game.

"Well—" Les said.

Edmonds appeared surprised. "I thought you'd take this as good news, Les."

"I do, sir."

"Then why are you so hesitant?"

"I'm not hesitant, sir."

But Edmonds was still frowning. "Then what's the matter?"

"It's just—it's just—" And here he almost told him. About what happened just before he came to Cedar Rapids. About the terrible thing that had happened when he had tried out as a pitcher for the Chicago White Stockings . . .

"Just what?"

Byron Fuller said, "Just that it's a big responsibility is what he means."

"Be quiet, Byron. I'm not talking to you. I'm talking to Les."

Fuller blushed and put his eyes down.

Les had never before seen the famous Clinton Edmonds temper.

"I have to say, I'm damned disappointed in how you've taken this news. This was supposed to be a happy occasion."

"Sir, I didn't mean to—"

"Let me finish, young man."

"Yes, sir."

"You are a citizen of this community and as such you owe it your absolute best. Am I right?"

"Yes, sir."

"Which means that whether it's marching off to war or pitching baseballs, you should respond with good spirits and pride. Am I right?"

"Yes, sir."

"Which means that you should look *forward* to any opportunity to better your community and make it an even more pleasant environment. Am I right?"

"Yes, sir."

Les glanced at Byron for some kind of moral support, but Byron was wisely keeping his head down. Halliman's eyes had gone out of focus.

"Do you know what it would mean to the people of this city if we were to beat Sterling? Do you?"

"Yes, sir."

"Are you old enough to remember the jubilation we had when General Lee surrendered?"

"Sort of, sir."

"There was literally dancing in the streets."

"Yes, sir."

"And that's what we'd have here."

"Yes, sir."

"Dancing in the streets."

"Yes, sir."

"So I'm going to ask you once again and I want your answer quickly. Do you understand?"

"Yes, sir."

"Are we going to beat Sterling?"

Les said, "Sir, we're going to beat their stockings off."

Clinton Edmonds smiled the smile of a very happy man. "Very good, Les. Very good."

But all Les could think of was what had happened at the Detroit Wolverines' training camp . . .

Byron, sighing, raised his head. Halliman's eyes came back into focus.

"Now, what say we each have a whiskey and do a bit of celebrating?" Clinton Edmonds said. "Does that sound like a good idea?"

Three grown men simultaneously tried to beat each other to saying "Yes!"

CHAPTER FIVE

Though there was only the one round of drinks, lunch went on till two.

At that point Halliman went back to his newspaper, second largest in circulation after the *Evening Gazette*, and the other three went back to the bank.

Les was scarcely across the threshold when he noticed the banner strung across the lobby of the bank. It read: ARE WE GOING TO BEAT DES MOINES? YOU BET!

Edmonds put a big hand on his shoulder. "Does that make you proud, son?"

Les knew how to answer. "Yes, indeed it does, sir!" he said, sounding like a drummer extolling the virtues of some miracle elixir. "Indeed it does!"

Edmonds patted him again. "That's how I like my answers, Les. Short and enthusiastic." He turned sharply to Byron Fuller. "Isn't that right, Byron?"

Byron snapped to attention the way he'd learned in military school. "That's *exactly* how you like them, sir. Short and enthusiastic."

Edmonds nodded to both of them and then strode back to his office.

Byron said, "I've got to admit something to you, Les."

"What's that—sir?"

Byron smiled. "It's just the two of us now. You don't have to call me 'sir.' Anyway, that's Clinton's idea, not mine." He leaned closer. "I've been sort of jealous of you."

"You have?" For a terrible moment, Les wondered if Byron had discovered the truth about him and Susan.

"Yes."

"But—why? I mean you're intelligent, you're well educated, you come from one of the best and oldest families in town and—"

"But I'm not a pitcher."

Les laughed out loud in relief. Baseball. That was all. "Oh, God, Byron—that's nothing."

"Well, if you would have heard Susan last night when she got back—"

"She wouldn't be any different about a track and field star or a football star."

"I'm not so sure. You seem to have caught her fancy. When we were growing up together, she used to taunt me about how much I liked sports. She'd never even go to a baseball game until—" He paused to think. "As a matter of fact, the first game she went to was this year. To see you pitch."

"Well, why don't you try out for the team yourself?"

Byron shrugged. "That's the problem. I'm tall, reasonably well-built, and I've certainly got the enthusiasm."

"Then what's stopping you?"

Now it was Byron's turn to laugh. "I'm missing only one thing, my friend."

"What's that?"

"Manual dexterity. I'm the world's clumsiest man."

And with that, Byron went to his office and Les to his teller station and the afternoon began.

Kids with freckles and kids with chocolate smeared over their faces and kids with bright pieces of straw between their front teeth lined the fence along the bottom of the bleachers watching another scrimmage game between the municipal team's first and second teams.

Behind them sat the adults. Word had spread quickly through the town that Cedar Rapids would play Sterling. Local citizens considered baseball second in sacred duty only to churchgoing. So the stands were filled. Rich men in fine-cut coats and silk ties sat side by side with workingmen in denim shirts and pants who, in turn, sat next to farmers from the periphery of the city. They sat in the last of the sunlight on sanded wooden boards smoking cigars and cigarettes and pipes and drinking three-cent glasses of sarsaparilla and champagne cider and birch beer. Most of the women drank a local favorite called the Spafizz. It cost a nickel. A few people let balloons go up against the blue sky. In six days, July 4, the game would be played and not even another war between the states would be as important as the forthcoming event.

Les Graves was on the mound.

By now, nearly six o'clock, he had faced ten batters. Four had struck out. Two had grounded out. One had walked. And two had flown out.

The eleventh batter now stepped to the plate.

Les, who had studied photographs of all the great pitchers, had spent two previous summers learning the vagaries of overhand pitching. At first he had considered overhand sort of feminine, but gradually he saw that you had more control and could throw more kinds of pitches.

He snapped one across the plate.

"Strike!" called the umpire.

The boys along the fence broke into a unison chant: "Les! Les! Les!"

The next pitch was also a strike.

This time the adults joined the kids in hollering Les' name.

Les smacked the ball into his glove several times before letting the next one go. His memories of the Chicago training camp were beginning to fade. He was older, he reasoned, and more experienced and what he'd done there, he would not repeat here.

As if to make his self-confidence conclusive, the ball sailed across the plate with speed so blinding that all the batter could do was jump back from the white flash so that he would not be injured.

The crowd roared.

Overwhelmed by the moment, Les looked in the direction of the little boys and waved his glove at them.

Yes, by God, he was going to take Sterling on and he was going to beat Sterling.

The rest of the game went quickly. Batters up, batters down. Five more strikeouts before it was all over.

Les joined his teammates in pouring beers from tin buckets brought from a nearby tavern.

The players sat on the grass, impending blue dusk splashed beautifully across the sky, and listened to Harding, the manager, talk as he paced up and down the length of them, beer foam on his upper lip.

"I don't have to tell you what the Sterling team has always said about us, do I?"

Everybody agreed that nobody here need be reminded of the various insults, both explicit and implicit, that Sterling had made about Cedar Rapids.

A hick town with hick players.

Overgrown schoolboys.

Not worth bothering with.

"And those are the things I want you to keep in mind as we get ready over the next six days," Harding said, walking back and forth. "They're going to come here on a fancy train car and they're going to make a big proposition out of the fact that one of their pitchers may be bought next year by the Cleveland Spiders and that two of their outfielders played for the Buffalo Bisons. And you know what?"

"What?" came a ragged chorus.

"We're not going to be impressed, that's what. And you know why?"

"Why?" came a fuller chorus.

"Because we're a better team. And there are some very good reasons for that." He paused to take a big swig of beer which seemed to bloat his already beered belly even as the men looked at him. "One, we hustle more. Two, we've got something to prove. Three, each and every one of us does his job. And four—" He splashed his mug in the direction of Les. "And four, we've got Les Graves!"

And then they were all waving their beers in Les's direction and yelling and hollering and screaming and acting exactly the way they gave their kids hell for acting.

Like goofuses.

Like crackerheads.

Like loons.

And having themselves a great time of it.

Thirty minutes later, pleasantly drunk, the men began to drift away to their homes.

Harding came up to Les and said, "Talk to you a minute?"

"Sure."

"Why don't we walk the bases. Nobody else needs to hear this."

"Fine."

So they walked the bases and smelled flowers and watched the moon come up and heard mothers calling children in from the night.

Harding said, "I'm just a fireman."

"Well, that's all right. I'm just a bank clerk."

"And Cedar Rapids ain't no goddamn Sterling and I'll be the first to admit it. We haven't got steam-driven trolley cars yet and we don't have telephones in a fourth of the homes."

Les was just drunk enough that he wondered if he was hearing Harding right. "You ashamed of us?"

Right there at second base Harding stopped and said (shouted really), "Hell, no, I ain't ashamed of us. I'm second-generation Cedar Rapids and damn proud of it."

"Then why—"

"Because that's what a lot of people in this town've got in the backs of their minds. That we're not as big and not as good. Well, I've got news for them."

Now Les, too, was caught up in Harding's angry spirit. He whirled around and threw beer up in the air and let it come down over his face, only a bit of it splashing into his mouth.

Then he caught sight of Harding, who was standing with his hands on his hips and staring at Les. Harding had lost his own enthusiasm.

"What's the matter?" Les said.

"I got something I need to say."

"Then say it."

"I'm half afraid to."

"Why's that?"

"Because I don't want to plant no doubts in your mind that ain't already there. If you follow me."

"I guess I do."

Harding cleared his throat and leaned back and gazed up at the starry sky. "It sure is a purty place we live in, Graves. Purty, purty, purty."

Well, Les thought, at least he's still drunk, which means there's at least half a chance he'll regain his good mood.

Then Harding's head snapped down and he said, "There's going to be a lot of pressure on you."

Les felt his stomach begin to tighten. "I know," he said.

"People are going to treat this like the most important event since the assassination of Abraham Lincoln."

"Clinton Edmonds sure is going to, anyway."

"Well, Clinton won't be alone."

"So I gather."

"And that's just it."

"What's it?"

"It don't matter."

"What doesn't matter?"

"Don't correct my English, smart boy."

"All right. What don't matter?"

"The game."

"The game," Les said, "don't matter?"

"No, it don't."

"But you just said—"

"I was sayin' what they think. Not what I think." He leaned forward and half glared at Les. "You ever tried to imagine eternity."

"Well, sure, I've tried—"

"Like yelling down a long wind—"

"Yes, something like that—"

"Well, in the scheme of things, that's about how important this game is."

"So it isn't important?"

"It's important that you don't think it's important."

"Huh?"

"The more important you think it is, the more pressure you're going to feel."

Les began to get Harding's point.

"So if you don't think it's important—"

"Then I won't get all tensed up—"

"And lose the game or nothin'."

By now they had completed the bases and stood on home plate.

"If you follow me," Harding said.

Les thought back to something Harding had said earlier. About not wanting to plant a seed of doubt where there hadn't been any.

But even by bringing up the subject of pressure, Harding only made Les remember all the more what had happened at the Detroit training camp—

Harding threw his arm around him and said, "I sure hope I didn't do it."

"Do what?"

"Plant no seed of doubt."

Les didn't want to hurt his feelings or scare him. He just said, in a half whisper really, "No, you didn't plant any seed of doubt."

And Harding burst out laughing again and said, "There you go again, smart boy, correctin' my English."

CHAPTER SIX

Neely leaned against the bar and looked around at the pitiable assortment of humanity.

This was mostly a worker's tavern and now at eight-thirty it was rolling toward that time of night when drunken wage earners did just what the entrepreneurs wanted them to do—fought among themselves. Neely was always mindful of Cromwell's ironic remark about defeating the Irish: "Just give them enough whiskey and they'll kill each other."

The tavern was a tribute to cheap pine, a long slab of which formed the bar behind which ran a mirror that had been cracked many times by hurled mugs and was presently held together by long strips of tape. It put you in mind of a badly wounded soldier. You could not say much more for the rest of the place, it being largely comprised of odors—cigar and cigarette smoke, urine from the outhouses, and sweat from the day's work. The biggest amenity was a fat Bohemian piano player with a farmer's red face and almost no skill at all on the keys. There were wobbly pine tables where some played cards but more spent time in pointless talk about baseball, and a few argued politics. There was a pool table which seemed to attract the serious attention of the few sober souls in the place.

And there were the women.

There was something about working-class girls that had always troubled Neely. He felt paternal toward them—wanted to say wash the rouge off your face and wear modest clothes and get yourself back to your pa's place—but his paternalism was a burden because he had learned a long time ago that he was not going to change the world.

Like T.Z., Neely had grown up in a poor German section of Chicago, where half the infants died before six months and where the cops were crooked and where a brutal army of thugs owned by a man named Allan Pinkerton broke the skull and spirit of any man who dared speak up for better living and working conditions.

There had been a time when Neely considered himself a radical—
he remembered what the radical T. Lizius, publisher of a Chicago
anarchist newspaper, said about Alfred Nobel's discovery of dynamite: "In giving dynamite to the downtrodden millions of the globe,
science has done its best work. The dear stuff can be carried around
in the pocket without danger, while it is a formidable weapon against
any force of militia, police or detectives that may want to stifle the cry
for justice that goes forth from the plundered slaves"—but that was
before the Halstead street riots, where Neely had seen the pointlessness of being a radical (just as he had come to see the pointlessness of
believing in the God of his youth). An army with rifles had opened fire
on a mob of unarmed railroad workers, who had only been asking
that the railroad (the impossibly rich railroad) not roll back wages any
more.

No, there was no point in it, and soon after Neely and T.Z. had
drifted into robbery as a means of supporting themselves. All you
could worry about in this universe was yourself and let the scabrous
parade of history, good and bad alike, pass by.

"Your friend's going to get his face smashed in if he keeps it up,"
said a voice to Neely's left.

Neely turned around and looked at a middle-aged worker with a
grimy face and dead right eye.

Amused, Neely said, "You don't imagine it would be the first time,
do you?"

"I s'pose not."

Neely followed the man's gaze to the back of the place where T.Z.,
who was dressed in his usual riverboat gambler attire (ruffled shirt,
string tie, colorful red silk vest, severely cut black coat), sat wooing a
working girl who looked just like all the working girls T.Z. usually
wooed—pretty and troubled. But then that could describe T.Z., too.
Because, despite a small scar beneath his right eye, he had the sort of
handsomeness that was almost beauty. And he certainly was troubled.

As he watched T.Z., Neely thought that when the time came to kill
him, he might actually be doing T.Z. a favor. For one thing, the man's
consumption was getting worse (he'd seen a doctor just last week), and
for another, his addiction to the bottle had robbed him of what
little common sense he'd had to begin with.

No, Neely needed T.Z. for only one more job, this one. And
then . . .

"She's Mike Dougherty's girl."

"Who's Mike?" asked Neely.

"Just the meanest bastard that comes in here."

"Where is he now?"

"Home probably." The worker nodded toward the girl with T.Z. "He goes home to his wife and kids, then sneaks back to see her."

"Sounds like an honorable man."

The worker scowled. "You wouldn't take that tone with him." And then, curiously, he broke into a smile. "And to prove it, here's Mike now."

If you judged him by looks alone, you would have to side with the worker that this Mike did *appear* to be, anyway, the meanest bastard in the bar.

He stunk of the preening bully. He was well over six feet, muscled in a fleshy but still firm way, and imposed himself on the scene around him by swaggering, glaring and carrying his right hand fisted, as if he were ready for anything instantly.

Everybody in the bar knew him and so they watched with inordinate interest as he made his way to the table where his mistress currently sat with T.Z.

The piano player stopped and the bartender started reaching for the ball bat bartenders always kept on hand.

"Just who the hell is this?" Mike said.

The girl, who was pretty in a sickly-kitten sort of way, said, "He's my friend."

"You're drunk," Mike said. "You know I hate it when you're drunk."

"I was just telling him how lonely I get."

At that, Neely had to smile. That, along with his looks, was one of the ways T.Z. had insinuated himself into so many beds. He loved sad tales—hell, he'd cry right along with his conquests—and so women always thought of him as a sympathetic listener.

"It's none of his damn business whether you're lonely or not."

T.Z. said, in a good rich baritone, "You shouldn't talk to her that way."

"You get the hell out of here and right now," Mike said.

"Maybe you'd better," the girl said.

"I won't have you talked to that way."

By now the crowd was fascinated. T.Z., slender, with long dark hair and the sleek manner of a big-city man, did not look like the kind of man who should be talking back to Mike Dougherty. (If any man should be talking back to Mike Dougherty.)

And Mike proved the crowd's assumption correct.

Faster than a big man should have been able to move, Mike reached down and grabbed T.Z. and jerked him to his feet.

He had cocked his fist and was about to let go when T.Z. sprang his own surprise.

He shot the sleeve of his right arm and in so doing placed a derringer right in the face of the meanest bastard in the tavern.

At this point, Neely moved fast.

They had work to do tonight and he didn't want it ruined by some tavern brawl, where the police got dragged in and T.Z. and Neely became familiar to them.

"You make one more move and you're dead," T.Z. said. T.Z.'s voice had the same kind of swagger in it that Mike's body had had a few minutes ago. T.Z. always felt very good about himself when he had a gun in his hand.

Neely went over and slid his arm expertly between the two men. He pushed them apart.

"Now, is this really worth pain and suffering for?" Neely said, sounding not unlike a priest. (Before he'd lost his faith, the year his three-year-old sister died of typhoid thanks to the Chicago sewer system, he had seriously considered being a priest.)

"He's with my girl."

"Merely talking to her," Neely said easily. "Merely talking."

"Then why's she bawling?"

Neely smiled. Looked about. "Is there a man here whom liquor has not turned into a melancholic?"

No man could deny Neely's truth.

"And that's all that's happened to your girl. The liquor saddened her heart."

"I'm going to sadden her face," said Mike. This got a laugh from the crowd.

"Can't I kill him, Neely?" T.Z. said.

Neely put out a hand.

Snapped a finger.

Put out the hand again.

T.Z. handed over the derringer.

"Wait outside," Neely said to T.Z.

"But—" T.Z. started to protest.

"Outside," Neely said.

As T.Z. left, reluctantly, Neely watched Mike Dougherty. The man obviously couldn't wait to get his hands on the girl. Neely could imagine those fists on the delicate bones of her face.

Neely, who had boxed for two years, stuffed the derringer in his jacket pocket and then ground a fist deep into Mike's solar plexus, followed it with a crashing punch to the man's temple and then finished things off by raising his knee brutally to Mike's groin.

The big man collapsed, smashing a pine chair on the way down.

To the girl, Neely said, "Do you have parents?"

"Yes, sir."

"Then go there. Stay there. Otherwise he's going to hurt you."

"I'm afraid."

"Hurry. Get home."

Neely waited till the girl had rushed out the door. Then he went to find T.Z.

"That wasn't smart," Neely said, jogging to catch up with T.Z., who walked down the street, in and out of the pools of lamplight.

"I get sick of you running my life."

"I figured you'd be mad."

"As I said, Neely, I'm tired of you running my life."

They came to a corner. You could hear and smell the river. From here you could see May's island, where the municipal buildings were.

Neely grabbed T.Z. by the sleeve and spun him around. "You forget. Thanks to your screwup on the train last April, they've got a description of us now."

"Of me," T.Z. snapped. "Of me. Not of you."

"I'm traveling with you. They might as well have a description of me."

"Anyway," T.Z. said, "it wasn't my fault the bandanna slipped off."

"No," Neely said, "it never is your fault, is it, T.Z.?"

Neely pulled his pocket watch out and held it up under the street-light. He sighed, getting hold of himself. He needed T.Z. for this one last job. Then it would be finished between them.

"It's time," he said.

"I hate to do this to the kid."

"It's already been settled, T.Z."

"He's changed. He's—"

Neely said, and his voice brooked no argument, "It's time, T.Z. It's well goddamn time."

CHAPTER SEVEN

Les Graves lived in a boardinghouse on the west side of the city in a section called "Time Check," so called because a bankrupt railroad paid many of its workers here with checks that took a long time to become cashable. People here came to be known as Time-Checkers.

The boardinghouse was a two-story, white-frame place with seven roomers in all.

As usual on summer nights, most of the roomers, four men and two women, were on the front porch. There was a table in one corner of the porch with a Rayo table lamp so you could play cards or read. Or you could join in the conversation, which usually ran to reminiscences of "older and better times" back on the farm, which is where most of the people came from, or about "newfangled inventions" (this being Mr. Weiderman, who worked at the three-story Grand Hotel downtown), or about Cedar Rapids history (if Mr. Waterhouse, who was an accountant at the Hawkeye Lumber and Mill Company, was talking; Mr. Waterhouse, it was said, was doing nothing less than writing a history of the town).

You could hear somebody stirring lemonade in the pitcher when Les reached the steps and you could hear Mr. Waterhouse saying, almost like a disembodied voice in the night, "Yes, sir, this town had its own steamship built back in 1858 and it docked in Cedar Rapids soon after. I can still remember the night—Roman candles and cannons firing and a brass band playing."

Les wished he could stay and hear the whole story because, the longer he was in Cedar Rapids, the more he loved the place and all the good high historical tales Mr. Waterhouse had to tell about it. (As Miss June Dodge, one of the other roomers, always said, "Mr. Waterhouse is the best entertainment in this town.")

But after muttering a hello he went directly inside and up the steps to his room to wash up and lie down.

Les had a Rayo lamp in his room, too, and when he got it lit, it

revealed a fairly large space with a sturdy single bed with a colorful
spread, a desk and chair, a shelf of books including virtually everything ever written by Sir Walter Scott, an outside photograph of
"Cap" Constantine, and a bureau with a mirror, a pitcher and a
washbasin. Les went down the hall, got some fresh water and then
came back and washed himself off, and then went and lay down on the
bed, closing his eyes so he could relax.

Night sounds came to him; a barn owl, a distant dog, a train headed
west with a lonely wail, the soft murmur of voices below in the summer evening . . .

He wasn't sure how long he'd been half asleep before a knock
came. A special gentle knock. So he knew it was the boardinghouse
owner, Mrs. Smythe, who was a widow.

"Les?"

"Yes?"

"You decent?"

"Just a minute, Mrs. Smythe."

He still wore trousers, so all he needed to do was grab a shirt.
"Come in."

She crept through the door. She bore in her fingers a small white
envelope. A note.

Les's heart pounded.

Mrs. Smythe, plump, dressed in her inevitable gingham and white
lace apron, said, "She left this for you earlier." Mrs. Smythe was a
very pretty woman with melancholy blue eyes that made her seem
younger than her fifty-some years.

"She?"

Mrs. Smythe looked at him. "You know who I mean, Les."

"Can I—can I see it?"

"Of course. It's *your* note."

She handed him the envelope.

Before he could open it, she said, "She's very beautiful."

"Yes, she is."

"I—" She started to say something but stopped.

"What, Mrs. Smythe?"

"Well, it's really not my business."

"We're friends, Mrs. Smythe. You can say what you like."

"Well, we had a talk, the lady and I."

"You and Susan?"

"Yes."

"What did you talk about?"

"Well, apparently, there'd just been some kind of blowup at her house and she'd come right over here to see you."

"What kind of blowup?"

"She wanted her fiancé to stand up for himself to her father but—"

"Oh, is that all?" Les said, relieved. "I thought maybe it was something between her and me."

At this point, Mrs. Smythe gave him a most curious look, and one Les would not forget for a while.

"What is it, Mrs. Smythe? What's wrong?"

"Oh—nothing. Just maybe we should have a talk sometime."

"About what?"

"About women."

"You mean about Susan?"

Mrs. Smythe smiled. "No. I'd say about women in general, Les."

"Can't we talk now?" Les was interested in what she might say.

"That note. She gave me sort of a hint as to what might be in it. She wants to meet you. In about a half hour." Mrs. Smythe turned back to the door. "I'd better be going now."

"I'd really like to have that talk."

Mrs. Smythe said, "She's a real lady, Les. You be good to her."

Then she was gone.

Forty-five minutes later, on the corner of Second Avenue and South Second Street, sat a black carriage just beyond the glow of the street-light. As he approached the carriage, Les could see a big sign that said, F. A. SIMMONS REAL ESTATE BROKER.

He went up to the carriage and peered in.

"Hello," Susan Edmonds said. "Would you like to go for a ride?"

"Sure."

As always when he saw her, he felt that uncomfortable mixture of excitement and fear—glad to see her, afraid that he would someday lose her.

He climbed aboard.

There had been no rain recently. The streets were dusty but very smooth. She handed him the reins and they set off. He'd been on such rides before and knew where to go. The edge of town.

He got glimpses of Susan in the moonlight. She wore a white

summer dress, lacy and with a high collar, and brooch at her throat. The brooch, he knew, had belonged to her maternal grandmother, her favorite.

"Mrs. Smythe said there was a scene at your house tonight."

"Yes," she said. "Yes, there was." She sounded worn.

"I'm sorry."

"So am I."

She started to cry.

"Is it—your father again?"

"Yes."

He didn't know what else to say. He repeated, "I'm sorry."

The horse moved smartly as the carriage rounded a bend filled with moonlight on dewy grass and pine trees. The smell was rich and deep and sweet, so much so that you wanted to get out and hold the pine in your hand and inhale it even deeper.

"He's so mean to Byron."

"I know."

"You do?"

"I've seen him at the bank," Les said. "He makes Byron jump."

"Byron doesn't deserve to be treated that way."

"Byron's a good man."

She looked at him. "You really mean that, don't you?"

"Sure. Why wouldn't I?"

"Some people would see Byron as their rival. I mean—our relationship and all—"

"Whatever our relationship, Susan, it doesn't alter the fact that Byron's a good man. He is."

"I think Daddy takes special delight in bullying Byron."

"Why?"

"Oh, because Byron's family is old money. His people came here at the time when the original settlers did from the East and the South. They had money before they got here, really, many of them. Daddy can't forget he's from the farm or that he wouldn't own a bank at all if there hadn't been that bank collapse back in '57 and he got it when it went into receivership. That's the funny thing. The wealthy people here have accepted Daddy and been very nice to him—it's Daddy who can't accept them—or himself."

"So he takes it out on Byron."

"Yes."

They reached a point where they always stopped and strolled along the river.

He sensed that tonight was not a good time to take her hand. That she was too troubled for romance.

They walked. On the air floated silver particles of fluffy dandelions and fireflies and pieces of dust motes in moonbeams. To their right the Cedar ran peacefully along and on the opposite shore a stand of white birches were like sentries in the night.

They came to a pavilion used for picnicking. He put his hands round her tiny waist and helped her up to sit on the edge of the cross beam so she could look down at the river.

"There's something I need to say."

Something in the way she said it made him pay special attention. He was so afraid of her impending words that he could scarcely breathe.

"All right," he said, barely able to talk.

Ever since he had held her note in his hands he had sensed she was going to say something terrible. Something—final.

"I've spent the past week thinking about us, Les."

"Me, too."

"I thought back to how we met. At that barn dance last spring. And how ever since we kept running into each other and how—without anything ever really happening—we seemed truly drawn to each other."

"I know."

"And I know I love you and I know you love me, but I think it's—" And then she stopped.

And he almost seized her to shake her so she'd find her thought.

"It's what?" he said finally.

"I think it's just loneliness."

"And not real love."

"Oh, no, real love. But a friendship kind of love, Les."

"Then you love—Byron—still?"

She took his hands and brought them together as if in prayer and then touched them to her cheek. "Yes, I do, Les." Then she frowned. "Or I would if he'd ever stand up to Daddy."

But he could hardly hear her.

His ears filled with the finality of her words.

He walked away from her, over to where the river rushed and shone silver. He stared at the water and thought how fine a dream it had been—his dream of somehow marrying Susan—but how he'd never been able to convince himself that it would ever actually happen.

He wanted to blame her but he couldn't. When he thought about it, all she'd ever talked about was her father and Byron, and how she wanted Byron to take his stand against his powerful would-be father-in-law. Only once had Les ever kissed her and that had been fleeting. She had needed someone to listen, a friend, and while that did not flatter his image of himself, he had to admit she had not led him on.

She came up and touched his shoulder. In the moonlight her small features and raven hair were lovely. "Have you seen May lately?"

He turned back to her. "No."

"You've been my friend, Les. Now let me be yours."

"It's all right, Susan," he sighed. "Why don't we just go back."

"No, please, Les. Let me say something."

"All right."

"I don't think you gave her a decent chance. She's a very nice girl."

"I know she's a nice girl."

"And I think— Well, I think pride kept you from loving her."

"Pride?" For the first time he allowed a note of anger in his voice. "What's pride got to do with it?"

"Men can be that way, Les. I know. Daddy's like that. If he thinks something's not good enough for him—well, it blinds him sometimes."

"I never said she's not good enough for me."

"No, you didn't say it. But I sensed it."

"She works in a hat shop and that's perfectly all right," Les said.

"It *is* perfectly all right. If only you'd believe that."

"Let's go."

"Les, I want us to part as friends."

"We're friends, Susan. Don't worry about that."

She stopped him and leaned forward and kissed him gently on the mouth. "I really care about you, Les. I want you to know that."

"Yes," he said, but it was a dull voice and seemed to belong to somebody else. "Yes, I know that."

Then they got in the carriage and went back.

On the porch, one of the roomers was saying to Mr. Waterhouse, "Tell us about that buried body again."

"Well," Mr. Waterhouse said, "it's getting kind of late."

"Please," said another boarder, "just that one and then we can all go to bed."

Les heard all this as he approached the porch and despite his mood —despite the fact that it was clear now he would never have Susan— he had to smile to himself. The boarders were like children whenever Mr. Waterhouse started telling Cedar Rapids stories. Please, just one more before bedtime, *please*.

"Well," said Mr. Waterhouse, "you know where the old distillery was. Well, on that site right there there's said to be a body buried— some say it was the result of two men fighting a duel over a woman, and others say it was over money and that the killer buried the body there and then bought the property next day so he'd have a private burial site."

Mr. Abernathy, who loved ghost stories, added, "And didn't you say once that people hear strange howlings there every once in a while?"

Mr. Waterhouse, who didn't believe in ghosts but who liked to keep his audience happy, said, "That's right, Mr. Abernathy. That's exactly right. Strange howlings every once in a while."

"My Lord," said Mr. Abernathy, absolutely thrilled. "My Lord."

Les muttered a "Good evening" to everyone and then went inside the vestibule.

Mrs. Smythe had the sliding parlor doors open so she could look up from the chair where she did her knitting and see who came in and out. "Les," she called when she saw him, "could you come in here a minute, please?"

He sighed, afraid she was going to ask him how it had gone with Susan. Right now, he didn't feel like talking.

"Good evening, Mrs. Smythe."

She nodded. "There's somebody in your room. Waiting."

"Who?"

"He didn't say. Just said it would be all right with you."

Still dazed from his time with Susan, all Les could do was shrug and say, "All right, Mrs. Smythe. Thanks for telling me."

He nodded, grateful that they hadn't talked about Susan, and then made his way back to the stairs. He was exhausted. First all the hoopla earlier today about the game and then tonight with Susan and—

He pushed open the door and looked in his room. He did not think that anything could shock him anymore today.

Yet now he stood there absolutely stunned.

"Hello," T.Z. said, standing up from the reading chair and putting out his arms. "I'll bet you're surprised to see me now, aren't you, boy?"

There was no doubt about that.

All Les could do was stand there gape-mouthed and stare.

It had been years since he'd seen his older brother, T. Z. Graves.

He had been hoping it would be years more before that dubious privilege came again.

He closed the door and went inside, and then T.Z. said, "Why don't you and me go for a walk, brother? Neely's waiting for us a few blocks down at a tavern."

Neely, Les thought. The coldest and most brutal man he'd ever known.

He looked with pity and contempt at his older brother—still dashing and handsome and slick. And still, as always, a criminal.

"Come on, Les. Me and Neely want to talk to you about something."

"About what?" Les said.

"Well, we just kind of want to see how you're doing, for one thing, in a nice little burg like Cedar Rapids. And for another, we want to talk to you about your job."

"What about my job?"

T.Z. smiled. "You got to admit, Les, it gives a couple bank robbers a pretty good edge when one of their brothers works in a bank."

T.Z. didn't stop laughing for a full minute about that one.

Then he said, "But you don't look too happy to see me."

"I'm not."

T.Z. glanced around the room. "You sure have gone respectable, Les."

"That was my intention."

"And I s'pect that's how most people in Cedar Rapids see you."

"How's that?"

"Respectable."

"Yes, I suppose they do."

"Good, then I won't spoil their impression of you unless you force me to."

"What's that supposed to mean?"

T.Z., in his riverboat gambler outfit, stood there and shook his head ironically. "Well, sir, I don't imagine folks around here would much take to the idea of somebody working in a bank if they knew he used to stick up banks himself."

T.Z. watched Les's face fall even lower and then said, "If you catch my meaning, Les. If you catch my meaning."

Half a minute later, they went to meet Neely.

CHAPTER EIGHT

Susan Edmonds stood outside the French doors looking in at her mother, who sat before the large fieldstone fireplace, with its patriotic decorations on the mantel, doing her knitting for the night.

The Edmonds house was a three-story wooden structure with a captain's walk and cupolas and spires that lent it a real grandness. The lawns sprawled a half mile in every direction and the livery was as big as many fine homes.

From upstairs came the sounds of Chopin on the summer night. Her eleven-year-old sister, Estelle, practicing for her recital the following week.

From the third-floor corner a light shone, which meant her father was working on books. He was obsessed with work. He had never forgotten his days as a poor farm boy. Her mother always said her father secretly dreaded that somebody would take from him all he'd earned.

Guiltily, she thought: At least when he's up in his study, he can't yell at us.

When her father was in one of his "moods," he was the sort of tyrant who made you twitch from nerves and made you tear up and fly from the room. The joke in town was that Clinton Edmonds owned such big grounds because he didn't want neighbors to hear him bellow. Susan spent her days walking around with her stomach in knots. Even when her father wasn't ranting, her dread of his doing so produced the same effects. He had done the same things to her two older brothers, both of whom, after college, had gone as far away as possible.

And now Byron was becoming just one more of her father's victims.

She closed her eyes, enjoying the Chopin and the faint glow of the fancy kerosene table lamps and the scent of mint from a nearby tree, and thought of her girlhood dreams of Byron.

He'd always been so handsome, yet never vain about it; he'd always been so manly (except when it came to sports, where he was so clumsy) and yet gentle, too. He'd gone East to school, to Dartmouth, and gotten the best grades possible in banking and finance, and then he'd returned here to work for her father. By then it was already assumed by Cedar Rapids society that Byron and she would be married. And indeed they were inseparable—going for canters on Sunday afternoon, attending concerts on Bandstand Hill in Bever Park, leading any other couples in tennis doubles, spending one or two nights a week at the Greene Opera House, where they both enjoyed the antics of such acts as Evans, Bryant & Hoey's (invariably billed as "A Tidal Wave of Merriment!") and a singer named Lillie Langtry who always brought her own company to perform a W. S. Gilbert comedy.

Yes, for the first three years following Byron's return, everything seemed wonderful. And her father treated Byron with deference, too. Susan sometimes suspected this was true because her father was intimidated by Byron's Dartmouth degree, her father scarcely having finished the eighth grade. But gradually this attitude changed and Byron slowly became just one more victim of her father's wrath and bullying until now—

Well, that's why Susan had sought solace with Les Graves.

Standing here now, opening her eyes and trying to give shape to the sprawl of stars that were the Big Dipper, she thought fondly of Les and wondered if she'd been selfish.

All she'd ever wanted from him was his friendship, but obviously, before she could do anything about it, Les made more of it than was there. One night, seeing the love in his eyes, she became frightened. She did not want to hurt him as she had been hurt all her life by her father and now by Byron, who was losing his integrity to her father . . .

She was thinking this when she was interrupted by a thunderous voice (she always thought of him as an Old Testament patriarch), one that automatically caused her to begin shaking and twitching . . .

Her father had stormed into the room and stood over her mother and shouted, "My best pen! It's gone!"

Her mother had already shriveled up in her rocking chair. "I didn't take it, Clinton! I know better than to touch your things!"

"No, you didn't take it! But you're so lax with that damn maid of ours that she can lose things without any fear of recrimination!"

"But Clinton, I—"

"You keep a terrible house, Arlene! A terrible house!"

And with that, he stormed out again, leaving in his wake two broken women and a troubled air that would linger for the rest of the night now and cause twitching and shaking, fits and starts of tears and anger that were utterly, utterly useless.

Susan hurried through the French doors now, to sit at her mother's knees, to comfort the woman she loved so much. The woman who had been living with this tyrant for four decades.

By the time she reached her mother, the gray-haired woman had lowered her head and was letting tears roll down her cheeks.

Even across the room she could hear her mother's whispered prayer and it was always the same prayer—one that asked not for any retribution against her husband, only that she be able to abide his rages and beratings with patience and charity.

Susan knelt next to the woman and cradled her head against her shoulder.

Neely said, "You've got a nice town here, Les. I hear there's an overall company that pays women twenty-five cents a day for ten hours' work."

T.Z. laughed. "I guess you probably remember that Neely here's a socialist."

"*Was* a socialist," Neely said with an edge. "Now I see that both sides are worthless."

The tavern was essentially a single long room with a long slab of pine for a bar and several kegs of beer hefted up into cradles behind the bar. There was sawdust on the floor. The only attempts at decoration were some faded posters depicting the "Wild, Wild West" as seen by everybody's favorite liar, Buffalo Bill Cody. The clientele appeared to be more drifter than workingman—rail-riders mostly.

"There's a table over there. Why don't we take it?" Neely said. "Talk about old times."

Les shook his head. "T.Z. told me why you're here. We don't have anything to talk about—old or new."

Neely smiled his shark smile and gazed ironically at T.Z. "See, he starts going out with a banker's daughter and right away he gets uppity."

Les had forgotten how clever Neely was. "How did you know about Susan?"

"Tonight, when you were at the river, you turned around and wondered if you hadn't heard somebody in the bushes." Neely laughed. "You did. It was me."

"You bastard."

"Your little brother sure doesn't seem glad to see us, T.Z."

"He'll calm down. Come on, Les. Let's go over and sit down and have a beer."

Les looked at his brother. As always he had the sense that the man was a complete stranger: his smooth, handsome face, his gambler's getup, and a certain constant anger in his dark eyes. They had been through so many years together, their mother dying when they were barely ten, and then their father going soon after, and Les struggling to get through high school while T.Z. (Thomas Zecariah) had drifted into one form of trouble after another, always coming back and asking his little brother to hide him out . . . and his little brother always accommodating him out of guilt and pity and fear. The night the old man died, Les had fallen asleep . . . it had been T.Z. who sat up with him and then first held the old man when he lay dying ("Don't close your eyes!" Les could remember T.Z. screaming, waking Les up) and then later it had been Les whom T.Z. had held, trying to comfort the sobbing and terrified boy . . . If only T.Z. could always have been the person he'd been at that moment.

"Come on," T.Z. said softly. He put a hand on Les's shoulder. "Even if you don't want to help us out, you can at least be nice to your brother, can't you?"

Les knew he was being manipulated. T.Z. was so good at that. His sad gaze. His gentle voice. His *need*. T.Z. could manipulate woman or man when he wanted to, and right now he wanted to.

Les nodded to the bartender for a beer, waited for his mug, and then picked it up and went over and sat down.

Neely said, "You like it here?"

"Cedar Rapids?"

"Yeah."

"Yes, I do."

"Actually, it looks like a nice-people little town."

"It is." It was difficult with Neely to keep a defensive tone from your voice. Neely always made you feel you had to apologize for existing. He was smart—smarter than most people, that was for sure —and he never let you forget it.

"Hey, Les, ease down. I'm not being sarcastic. I spent the day walking around. You didn't see me—but I was there when you were pitching that scrimmage game and I—well, I was there when you went for a ride with Susan."

Before Les could get angry again, T.Z. said, "So you're pitching again?"

"Yes."

"Too bad that had to happen and all. In Chicago, I mean."

"I just got—scared."

For once T.Z.'s smile seemed genuine. "You were like that when you were a little kid. You'd want something and then just before you got it—you got scared. Like you didn't deserve it or something." T.Z.'s voice was not without a certain sadness. "Where me—I just took the things I wanted."

Neely said, "I'm really happy that you two want to talk about the old days. But we're here on business, T.Z." He looked at Les. "T.Z.'s wanted for murder."

T.Z. slammed his fist on the table. "God, Neely, you promised—"

"The kid should know the truth."

Les just sat there, stunned. "Murder?"

He had long ago accepted the reality of his brother being a thief. But T.Z. and Neely usually managed to keep their robberies to small-town banks and to cheating traveling businessmen out of their money and working vast scams on groups of greedy suckers.

"What happened?"

"Train," Neely said.

"You stuck up a train?"

"Yes," Neely said, and for the first time he sounded defensive.

"God," Les said. "You know all the trouble that goes with that."

Neely leaned forward. "Well, your brother let his mask slip. I thought I'd killed the only man who could identify him, but somebody else saw us as we escaped—" He pulled a folded-up sheet of paper from his pocket. Handed it to Les. It was a WANTED poster. $5000 Cash was being offered by the railroad for the apprehension, Dead or Alive, of this man for whom the poster had no name. Fortunately for T.Z., at the time he was seen escaping the train, he'd been wearing a beard.

"But you just said you killed him," Les said to Neely.

"I did. But it doesn't matter which one of us actually killed him. We'll both hang if they catch us."

"We need money," T.Z. said. "We need to go to Mexico. Hide out there for a few years."

"What about the money from the train?"

A cruel smile touched Neely's lips. "T.Z. here seemed to be of the mind that a certain diamond shipment was being sent from Chicago to Sterling." Neely shook his head. "Seems T.Z. was wrong."

"We didn't get much of anything," T.Z. said.

"Then we heard from Dubbins—remember him? He happened to be riding the rails when he spotted you in Cedar Rapids. Working in a bank no less," Neely said. "So—we came here to see you." He leaned forward, half whispered, "We figured the way we covered for you the last time you worked in a bank, you'd be more than willing to help us out."

"I only took that money because we had to pay off that doctor."

T.Z. had been wounded in a failed attempt to rob a telegraph station. By the time they reached the small Nebraska town where Les had been working, T.Z. was nearly dead. There was a doc who'd fix him up and not report him to the law—for $500. None of them had the money, so Les was forced to pilfer it from the bank where he'd been working. Then he had to flee town with them before he was caught.

Now they were here again, dragging him once more into their web of failure and violence.

And now murder.

"I can't do it," Les said.

"He's gone too respectable, T.Z.," Neely said coolly. "You see, that's what's wrong with the capitalist system. You take Les here. Sure, he loves his brother. Sure, he's grateful his brother helped raise him after the old man died. But now he's got this comfortable job making comfortable money and seeing the banker's daughter on the side—so he has to weigh one thing against the other—the things capitalism has given him against his love for his brother. And capitalism wins every time."

By the time he'd finished speaking, there was real ire in his voice and his burly body shook with anger.

"You can go to Mexico," Les said to T.Z. "I'll start sending you a part of my paycheck."

"Won't that be nice, now," Neely said. "Two or three dollars a month, I'd bet."

"I'd send you everything I could," Les said to T.Z., disregarding Neely. "I promise."

Neely sighed. For the first time his battered face looked dusty and old. He seemed weary. "You always were a little naive, Les. You don't understand this. The federal boys are dogging our tracks day and night. It's just a matter of time. We need the money in the next couple of days. And we need to head for Mexico right away."

"He's not exaggerating, Les. He's really not."

"I just can't do it."

Neely waved for another round. "I'll tell you what, Les. Before you say yes or no, just listen to our plan. That's all we're asking you to do. Just listen. Because I think you'll see that you can help us without anybody ever knowing. All right?"

T.Z. said, softly, "All right, Les? Just listen. All right?"

So the next round of beers came.

And Les, of course, listened.

CHAPTER NINE

In the summer streets you could hear the sound of great and earnest hammering, as if some colossal monument were being built.

Actually, it was many monuments—floats for the Fourth of July parade three days hence.

On his way to work, Les went down an alley to an open area behind the Empire Hotel. In the morning sunlight, on a field of deep green grass, young people laughed and chattered but kept working diligently at their tasks—making from paper and papier-mâché tributes to the the Civil War, to the rich Iowa farmland and to dozens of local merchants—there was a banner for Turechek's grocery store; a big shoe inside of which would stand a waving girl for Lyoran Brothers shoe store; a large depiction of several kinds of baked goods for the C. K. Kosek bakery; and there were at least fifteen more.

As he watched them, Les felt an unlikely envy. He wished he were one of these kids—an eighteen-year-old boy flirting with a cute city girl as they worked side by side toward the lazy summer's biggest event. Looking forward to stolen kisses in the prairie moonlight . . .

But he had a slight hangover and was still tired as he recalled last night talking to T.Z. and Neely . . .

And his innocent images of innocent romance faded as he recalled how he'd stolen to save his brother's life . . . and how they were using his stealing against him now—

So he could help them take the money from Clinton Edmonds' bank.

He stood a few more minutes watching the sunlight dry the dew on the grass, watching glue being slopped on papier-mâché, watching two-feet-tall letters being measured out so they could be painted in—

And then he turned away.

He was too old and had been too many things to appreciate this sort of innocence anymore.

Even baseball, which had once been his favorite pastime, had become a burden. When he thought of the headaches he'd developed during the spring training camp in Detroit . . .

He hurried on to work.

Byron Fuller said, "Morning, Les." He was passing on his way to his office, but then he stopped and came back. "Are you all right?"

Les nodded.

"You look—sick, or something."

"I guess I've got a headache, sir."

Byron smiled. "Nobody's around, Les. Remember, you don't have to call me sir."

He stared at Byron, thinking again how good it would be to dislike —even hate—the man whom Susan Edmonds loved. But he couldn't . . .

Byron said, "Why don't you go in the washroom and throw cold water on your face."

"I'm all right. Really—"

"I know. But you want to look as wide awake as possible for when Clinton sees you. Otherwise he'll get afraid that you won't be all right for the game."

"Well—"

Byron sighed and then sort of whispered. "You know how he is, Les. He can sort of—well, beat you down."

Just as he's beaten you down, Les thought. And Susan. And me.

Les smiled briefly. "It's kind of strange how people get so powerful, isn't it?"

Byron nodded. "What's even stranger, Les, is how power affects some people to do good things and other people—well, some people just can't seem to handle it." Then he flushed and realized he was saying something terrible about his own future father-in-law. "Of course, I wasn't talking about Clinton."

Les laughed. "No, of course not."

Byron's face was still red. "Well, I'd better be getting on to my office. Hope you feel better."

"Thanks, Byron," Les said and meant it. He felt that for the first time in two years of knowing each other, of being polite to each other, they'd finally said something that touched on reality, their shared fear and disgust with the tyrant Clinton Edmonds.

The morning went quickly.

The city streets were filled with wagons and carriages bringing provisions in and taking provisions out. Through the big plate-glass window, Les could see that the sidewalks were jammed with farm families getting ready for the holidays—making the sweep down First Avenue, then over past the Granby Building that held a myriad of small businesses and shops, then down Third Avenue with its variety of colorful awnings to offer customers shade from searing sun and a roof from pounding rain.

Clinton Edmonds came over only once that morning. As most people in the bank knew, he was negotiating to purchase a small bank in a nearby town called Tipton. He was preparing for a visit this afternoon. So, fortunately for Les, Edmonds seemed somewhat distracted when he slapped a beefy arm around him and said, "We're going to make fools of that Des Moines team, aren't we?"

In the most enthusiastic voice he could summon, Les said, "We sure are, sir!"

Placated, Edmonds moved on, eventually back to his office.

George Buss leaned over and said, "You're going to get a promotion out of this game. You just wait and see." Being George, he said this completely without envy. He was just awed by the process of how the world's wheel really turned.

Les spent the last hour before lunch glancing up at the big Ingram watch just above the front door. He had already decided where he was going to go over the lunch hour and he was beginning to feel some urgency about it.

Wolf's Millinery stood on the corner of Third Street South East.

At noon time the streets were crowded with downtown workers shopping and with customers from outlying areas coming into town via buggies and the streetcars.

Les stood in front of the millinery window peeking inside for sight of May Tolan.

Presently all he could see was the north wall of the place, where large glassed-in cases with sliding doors displayed what seemed like hundreds of large hats with huge (sometimes overwhelming) floral ornaments, of the sort popular this year.

In front of the cases were mahogany stands where even more hats were shown.

Ladies in pairs and trios walked up and down the aisles of the place, trying on various hats—some evoking admiring smiles among their friends, some (the gaudier kind) eliciting smiles if not downright smirks, and still a few more puzzlement. There was one hat off which spilled enough grapes to start a vineyard. Who would wear such a thing?

Finally, still unable to find May anywhere (and then suddenly fearing that she, too, might be on her lunch hour), Les started around to the front of the place.

And that's when he saw Neely.

The big Irishman, looking like a roughneck version of a banker himself in his three-piece suit and string tie, leaned against a shop a hundred feet away smoking his hand-rolled cigarette.

He walked over to Les with his easy gait, its very easiness suggesting a self-confidence that was really arrogance.

"You're following me, aren't you?" Les said. He had begun to sweat. He was angry. He also felt, as the tightness of his stomach attested, fear. He had known Neely for twenty-five years and had never been able to understand the man. Neely was the sort who got tears in his eyes when little kids hurt themselves by falling down or getting sick. He had a real sympathy for life's injured and wounded. But he had also seen Neely kick in a man's ribs until the man started bleeding out of his mouth, nose and ears. Les and T.Z. had had to haul Neely off the man. Neely made no sense to Les and that made him not only inscrutable but totally dangerous, like a weapon that could be set off at any time.

"Sure. I remember you when you were a little kid," Neely said. "You liked to wander around—get lost." He smiled. "I'm just making sure you don't get lost."

"I'm not going to do it, Neely. What you proposed last night."

Neely just kept on smiling. "Sure you are."

"You can't force me."

"Of course I can."

"I don't give a damn who you tell about my past."

Neely's eyes narrowed. "It isn't your past you've got to worry about now, Les. It's your brother's past. Don't forget that T.Z. is wanted for murder."

You could see by Neely's eyes that he had succeeded in rattling Les.

"They'd hang him and you know it."

"They'd hang you, too."

"If they caught me. Remember in the old neighborhood, Les—I always came out on top. T.Z. rarely did."

Les sighed. "I—I'm trying to start a new life here, Neely. I don't expect you to understand that. But that's why I kind of—retreated back here. To start again. And now—"

Neely took a deep drag on his quirly and tipped his hat with the broad gesture of a gentleman to a pretty bonneted young woman passing by in the fine lovely June sunlight.

Then Neely turned back to Les. "If you do it just the way we told you, nobody will ever know you had anything to do with it."

"But, Neely—"

"You ever see a man hang, Les? They hung my uncle."

"Neely, I know—"

"My old man never got his brother's screams out of his head. Even on his deathbed my old man was crying about what it had been like to see his brother die—"

"Neely—"

"It'll be like that with T.Z. and you know it. He isn't strong, T.Z. isn't. Not strong at all, kid, and you know it."

Les sighed. All he could think of to say was "Don't follow me around anymore, all right?"

Neely smiled. "Just wanted to make sure you didn't get lost, kid."

"And don't call me kid anymore, either."

Neely flicked his quirly into the gutter. "All right, Les. I don't want to make you unhappy." Then his eyes became slits in the sunlight and he said, "I'll see you tonight, Les. Tonight." Then he was gone.

Before he entered the millinery store, Les had to go around the corner and get his composure back.

People passing him on the street looked at him closely, as if he were sick or something.

Finally, after a few minutes, he took several deep breaths, said something that resembled a prayer and then went back around the corner and into the millinery store.

A bell tinkled as he entered the long, narrow shop and almost immediately a large woman in a yellow, bustled dress appeared and said, "Yes, sir, may I help you?"

Les gulped and said, in a voice that sounded none too confident, "I'd like to see May Tolan."

And then, in the back of the store, stepping out from between parted curtains, he saw her.

As always she looked lovely in a delicate and somewhat nervous way, her auburn hair pulled back in the sort of loose bun called a chignon. Her particular kind of prettiness reminded Les of a small kitten not quite able to cope with the world of giants surrounding it. She walked slowly toward him now, graceful in a simple tan frock, her grave brown eyes looking excited and afraid and even a bit angry all at once.

The other woman, sensing the personal nature of the business, said, "I'll be in the back, May dear."

May nodded.

Les said, his voice shaking, the first stupid thing that came to mind. "Been a while, I guess."

Levelly she said, "Four months."

"I've been meaning to get hold of you."

"Could you help me with this?" an important-looking woman interrupted.

"Of course," May said.

As he watched her, Les wondered if she ever resented it. She was so much more elegant than many of the women she waited on—yet so many of them treated her with the contempt of the wealthy.

By the time she had finished with the first woman, several others had come into the shop, tinkling the bell, waiting impatiently to be served.

Les had prepared so many words his head ached with the press of them all—but he could see now he would not have the opportunity he needed to say them to her. Not here.

Les just stood there, bowler in hand, trying to look comfortable despite the scrutiny of half a dozen women who were obviously wondering what a *man* was doing here.

The woman in yellow came back. She said, in a discreet voice, "You're not here to see May on business?"

"No, I guess I'm not."

"Well, May is very busy. This isn't a good time."

"Yes. I—I guess I can see that."

"I can take a message for her if you'd like."

"No, no message. But—could you tell me when she has her lunch hour?"

The woman frowned. "I was going to suggest that you stop back then—but I'm afraid it may be two o'clock at the rate things are going."

Two o'clock. Les would be back in his teller station. "All right. Why don't you just tell her that I'll see her later, then."

"Fine. Sorry you didn't get a chance to see her." The woman, surprisingly, did not seem sorry.

"Oh, that's all right."

As he left, May was fitting a hat to a woman's head. But he could see, around the angle of the ornamenting floral design, her brown eyes watching him.

Sadly.

And then it came back to him—her grief the night he'd told her that he did not want to see her anymore—how instead of tears a distance had come into her eyes, a distance he could not stand to watch, a distance far worse than words or anger could ever have been.

He saw some of that distance in her gaze now.

And he hurried out of there.

CHAPTER TEN

"He was rude to you."

"It's just his manner."

"You're afraid of him."

"I'm just polite."

"He humiliates you and you let him."

"As I said, Susan, it's just his manner."

In the center of the downtown was a square of summer green grass with park benches and tables where many of the merchants and their employees sat and ate their lunches watching pigeons trundling around and dogs chasing after them. The city groundskeeper showed some of his most beautiful snapdragons, petunias and roses in a small but famous garden here and the air was rich with its blessings.

Susan sat across the table from Byron Fuller. She had brought them a picnic basket with chicken sandwiches and ice tea and two slices of chocolate cake for his noon hour. She liked festivities, so she also spread out a red and white checkered tablecloth that was brilliant in the daylight.

For the first ten minutes she had stopped herself from mentioning last night—how her father had exploded at Byron over some innocently expressed political opinion (Byron was not a particular admirer of President Arthur's) but Byron had not defended himself at all.

But then he had never defended himself in all the years that Clinton Edmonds had been browbeating him—and Susan was beginning to lose respect for Byron. Which was why, of course, she'd turned briefly to Les Graves.

"I need to say something to you, Byron."

"You know," Byron said, in his best calm voice, "I read an article in *Harper's Weekly* a few issues ago which said—"

"I don't give a damn what it said."

Byron blushed and looked quickly around to see if any of the other people in Greene Square might have heard her use profanity.

"My Lord, Susan," he said.

"I just want you to understand the gravity of this lunch today."

"I just don't see what you're so upset about."

"I'm upset because my whole future is at stake."

"I don't know what you're talking about."

"If my father breaks you the way he broke my brothers—we'll never have any peace as husband and wife. He'll run our lives because you'll let him."

"I most certainly will not let him run our lives." For the first time Byron sat up straight and seemed touched by something resembling pride.

"Then the next time he shouts at you or tries to humiliate you—stand up to him."

"But he's—"

"He's what?"

"He's your father."

"He also happens to be a tyrant."

"And he's—"

"What?"

"He's—my elder. You're supposed to have respect for your elders."

"You heard me, Byron. He's destroyed the lives of my mother and my brothers, but I'll be damned before I let him destroy my life!"

Byron leaned forward and stage-whispered, "Will you please quit using profanity! *I'm a banker*—what will people think?"

"Right now I don't care what people think."

His stage whisper continued. "Well, I do care. I have to care. *I'm a banker.*"

She smiled. "You look so cute right now, Byron. You're so embarrassed and helpless—like a little boy." She knew she loved him at moments like these. Without trying in the least, Byron was so winning, good, kind and gentle and patient, just as he'd been all the years they'd grown up together. Sometimes he was her lover and sometimes her friend and sometimes he was even her own little boy, deeply in need of help in a world far more cynical than he ever imagined it to be. She prayed, literally on her hands and knees, that her father would not destroy Byron with his own virtues.

"It seems I should ask you a question," Byron said.

"Which would be?"

"Which would be—do you love your father?"

She thought a long moment. "Yes; yes I do. And I also understand him. I understand that because of his background he does not feel secure in the company of people he considers his betters—you, for instance."

"Me?"

"Of course you. You and your family."

"But he's the richest man in town."

"He didn't even finish high school."

Byron sighed. "I know you're right, Susan. About his feeling insecure. You can see it in his eyes whenever we have a board meeting. Here are these pompous lawyers and factory owners sitting around and at the head of the table is your father, and unless he's yelling at them he seems—unsure of himself."

"Exactly."

"So I wouldn't judge him too harshly. We all have faults."

"You're afraid of him, aren't you?"

Byron sighed again and averted his eyes. "I suppose I am. A little."

"I need to say something, Byron."

"What?"

Now it was her turn to lean closer. "If you don't stand up to my father, you'll lose me."

"But, Susan—"

"I want to be married to a man who has enough pride in himself to defend himself."

"Please, Susan, please don't talk like that. About me—losing you."

"It's true, Byron."

"But—"

"I've lived with my father's tyranny all my life. I want my own home to be very different from the one I grew up in. I don't want it controlled by my father's rages and whims."

He set down his chicken sandwich and looked glumly at his plate. "The article was right."

"What article?"

"The one I tried to tell you about in *Harper's Weekly*. It said you should never try to eat when you're upset. It says it makes good digestion impossible." He touched his stomach. "I know this is an impolite thing to say, Susan, but I'm afraid our whole conversation has given me gas."

"Oh, God, Byron," Susan said, laughing. "Sometimes you really are my little boy, aren't you?" Then a frown claimed her mouth and she said, "But I'm serious, Byron. You either stand up to him or—"

Byron's face showed the panic he felt. "Don't say it, Susan. Don't say it ever again. I—" He touched his heart. "I've never felt the way I'm feeling right now. Never."

There were tears in his voice.

The beauty of the day was lost suddenly on both of them.

Around three o'clock that afternoon a priest walked into the bank where Les Graves worked and stood for a considerable time at the desk where you made out deposit slips.

To anybody who was paying attention to the priest, it was easy to see that the man only occasionally wrote anything on his slip. Instead his hard blue eyes surveyed the bank and how it was laid out.

Neely had learned long ago that, as with any uniform, what people remembered was the uniform itself and not the man.

So he took his time.

The plan he'd laid out to Les last night was one he'd heard about in Ohio, when he'd done a three-week stint for drunk and disorderly.

The plan, when you thought about it, was about the most foolproof way there was of taking money from a bank without anybody being the wiser for at least twelve hours.

The trick was that one of the robbers had to be a bank employee.

It was even better, Neely smiled to himself, when one of the robbers was related to a bank employee. But to ensure Les's cooperation he had to unsettle him. Which was why Neely was here.

For the next ten minutes he kept up the ruse of making out a deposit ticket, looking very officious while he was at it.

He saw the teller stations and the offices on the facing wall. The offices interested him. For a closer inspection he had to go up to one of the stations and ask for information.

"Good afternoon, Father," said the plump woman behind the barred window.

"Good afternoon. I was wondering if you could tell me—I must be getting forgetful in my old age—I was wondering if you could tell me what the date is."

"You're hardly getting old, Father," the woman said, and laughed. "At least I hope not. I forget the date all the time and I'm barely twenty-five. Now, does that make me old?"

"It certainly does not," the priest laughed back, doing his best to keep his eyes from her wonderful breasts. Ogling her would hardly be the priestly thing to do.

And anyway, he had other things to look at.

Neely had selected the last of the teller stations so he could look into the glassed-in offices and see how they were laid out.

It took him less than half a minute to see that none of them would be of much use.

"July 2 is the date, Father."

"Oh, yes, how could I forget, with the Fourth coming up."

"The Fourth and our big baseball game against Des Moines."

"That's right," the priest smiled. "That's right."

He continued to talk to the woman so he could keep surveying the bank.

Then he saw a man with a green eyeshade and a red arm garter carrying a stack of ledgers come around a corner at the far end of the offices.

Neely had not considered the possibility that there was another area to the bank he had not seen.

Quickly, he decided to take a chance. "Could you direct me to a men's facility?"

"Why, of course, Father. You go down to the end of the offices and take a right."

"Thank you very much."

"You're quite welcome, Father."

Neely nodded to the woman and moved away from the station, careful that his thick eyeglasses had not slipped too far down his nose.

As he passed the offices, he glanced in at each. He liked to memorize a place in advance so there were no surprises when the time came to rob it.

Then he came to the final office and went right. There was a narrow hallway that led eventually to a back door that was barred and locked. But before reaching the back door you passed a large open office where several bookkeepers worked and then another smaller office that appeared to be a kind of lounge for employees.

Near the back door were two smaller doors marked, respectively, MEN and LADIES but it was the door between them that interested him.

He paused here, careful to see that nobody was watching.

He moved quickly.

He had just put a hand on the middle door when a voice said, "I think you have the wrong door, Father."

Neely spun around as if somebody had shot him.

There stood a handsome but somewhat pompous-looking young man who said, "I'm Byron Fuller, vice president of the bank, Father."

He put out a hand.

Neely shook it.

"I assume you wanted the men's."

"I did indeed." Then he pulled back his head and squinted. "I seem to be lost—"

"That's a storage closet there, Father. You want the door next to it."

Neely smiled. "The good Lord has granted me many things, but good eyesight, alas, is not one of them."

Byron Fuller smiled. "Quite all right, Father. Quite all right. Good day."

Then Byron went back into the accounting department.

Now Neely had to move extremely quickly.

He put his hand on the door of the storage closet and eased the knob open.

From the darkness inside came smells of sweet floor polish and the dust collected on mops.

He stuck his head inside, eyes quickly adjusting to the gloom. From what he could see, the closet was at least six feet deep.

About the size of a cell—

He shook his head, ridding himself of the thought, and then quickly closed the door again.

He went back up to the front of the bank. He had decided to have some fun, the sort of teasing fun that he enjoyed.

He filled out a deposit ticket and then went over to a teller station.

The bank was busy again with red-faced farmers and housewives in bustled dresses and sun-scorched day workers who were putting up telephone poles.

So Neely had to wait in a line that was four deep before he got the satisfaction and slid the deposit ticket through the opening in the teller cage.

Les Graves had been working very quickly. Hardly noticing the customers he waited on.

But now his head jerked up and his eyes sought the face of the priest with the small eyeglasses.

And then a terrible recognition dawned in Les's eyes.

And Neely smiled.

He glanced down at the note he had just handed Les.

It read: THIS IS GOING TO BE AN EASY PLACE TO ROB.

Then Neely left, a pale and shaken Les standing behind at his teller station.

CHAPTER ELEVEN

The man had been asking questions since just before noon, a few minutes after he stepped down from the Chicago, Burlington and Quincy line at 11:07 A.M.

The man had three questions and he asked them of several shopkeepers along Third Avenue, and then, not getting any satisfaction, he went over to First Avenue and started asking questions there.

He was a fat man in a three-piece brown suit that was wool and too hot for the eighty-degree temperature. If you looked closely, on his lapels you could see faint traces of cigar ash. The man loved stogies. His face did not seem to belong to his body, solemn and angular. Given its gauntness, it belonged on the face of a thin man. His hair, which was thinning, was pressed wetly with sweat to his scalp, which was almost a rust color. The man was an Indian. Then there was the rest of him. He had short arms that made his huge girth seem even more comic. His hands, however, were anything but comic. Even the untutored eye could see where his knuckles had been broken many times. They were brutal hands, broad and flat and strong.

He stood now and said to a merchant, "His name is Les Graves."

"Les Graves?" the merchant said. He ran what was called a stationery store and it sold just about everything you could want in pens and pencils and writing paper, plus it had a whole wall of bright-colored books, including a new one by Robert Louis Stevenson called *Treasure Island.* "Why, heck yes, I know Les Graves." The man laughed. "Best pitcher this town ever had."

The man did not permit himself to show excitement. "Pitcher?"

"Sure. On our municipal baseball team. Big showdown with Sterling on the Fourth."

"So you know where I could find him then?"

"Sure do."

The fat man smiled. "And where would that be?" He said it a little breathlessly. It could have been because of his repressed excitement or it could have been because his weight always made him sound a little breathless.

"Why, just around the corner. At the bank."

The fat man's eyes got very bright. "I'd certainly like to thank you, sir."

For the first time, the merchant seemed a bit suspicious. "You, uh, looking for Les for any particular reason?"

"Oh, no," the fat man said equitably enough. "No real particular reason you might say." He paused and smiled. "Just a friend of his. From the old days."

The merchant seemed relieved. "Well, just go right over to the bank and say hello to him then. And I hope you get to stick around for the game day after tomorrow."

"Yes," the fat man said, "yes, I've got a feeling I'll be doing just that."

Then he tipped his bowler and went back outside into the steaming heat of the afternoon.

Two hours later, Les got suited up in one of the bank's back rooms and then walked over to the ballpark for practice.

The stands were filled again. It was as if the game itself were only moments away.

Harding, the manager, came over and said, "I want you to take it easy today."

"I will."

"Don't throw no fancy stuff, either. Save that for Thursday."

"Don't worry."

As they stood there, Les became aware of how closely Harding was watching him. "You didn't get any sleep last night, either, did you?"

"Not much."

"You look bad, Les. Tired."

"I'm fine."

"Hell, Les. What's going on?"

"Nothing."

"I thought we were friends."

"We are."

"Then tell me."

"There's nothing to tell," Les said. "I'm fine."

Harding spat tobacco juice from a lump in his left cheek and said, "Get out there and play ball."

Les nodded and ran out on the field. By the time he'd reached the mound, the stands had gone wild applauding him.

When he turned around, his eyes naturally fell on the three people sitting in the box seats behind the home plate—Clinton Edmonds, his daughter Susan and Byron Fuller.

The catcher was putting the rubber in his mouth—some catchers wore a rubber protector the way boxers did—and then he tossed a clean white ball out to Les.

Of the first three pitches, two went wild to the side and one went up so high, the catcher had to leap in the air to bring it down.

All Les could think of was what had happened a few years back when he'd tried out for Chicago.

"You'll be all right," the catcher called out to him. "You just got to concentrate the way Harding always tells us."

That was Harding's favorite word.

Concentrate.

So Les took the ball and did the best he could on concentrating. It wasn't easy—not when images of his brother hanging from a gallows filled his head.

No, sir, it wasn't easy at all.

Many people noted the fat man's passage to the bleacher way at the top. He moved with the difficulty of a boat in troubled waters.

By the time he reached the top, his cupid's face ran with sweat and his celluloid collar was yellow with sweat.

For the first few minutes he took off his hat and fanned himself. A plump black crow swooped down and sat next to the man, watching him. The man, annoyed with the bird, struck him with his hat. The crow flew away.

Finally, finished fanning himself, the man turned his attention to the field below.

He did not like games. They bored him. Still, there was something exciting about the sight of nine men in clean white uniforms in the field and a park full of rooters cheering them on. The few times he'd gone to see the Chicago White Stockings, boys had passed among the spectators, with the boxes filled with various kinds of food for sale—sort of like a traveling cornucopia. The boy who worked his way up the aisle seemed to be selling only one thing. Some kind of semi-lemonade concoction. The fat man bought two of them.

Then he went back to looking at the field.

Even from here, even without the help of field glasses, he could see the resemblance between the man he sought and the man on the pitcher's mound.

The pitcher was not so good-looking as the brother—the brother being almost pretty—but the resemblance was indeed unmistakable.

The pitcher was not having a good day and this led the fat man to wonder why so many of the townspeople made such a fuss over his pitching.

Thus far the fat man had watched him face three batters. Two of them he'd walked and one of them had gotten a single. The crowd did not seem disappointed so much as confused, as if they didn't quite know what to make of what they were seeing.

A luxurious breeze came and dried the rest of the sweat on the fat man's face. He could smell the nearby river and newly mown grass and the sweet smell of cigar smoke lazing up from the bleachers below.

In all, nine batters came to the plate before the top half of the sixth inning was over. Two runs had been scored. The pitcher looked disgusted and faintly embarrassed as he left the field. By now the fat man had figured out that the pitcher was playing against his own second team and the second team's pitcher looked better than he did.

The kid with the cold drinks came by again and the fat man bought two more.

There were three more innings and the way young Graves was pitching, they promised to be long ones.

In the reserved box seats below, Clinton Edmonds, red-faced and angry, waved the manager Harding over.

Harding came running. He wore the face of the eternal supplicant, the gladiator prostrating himself before the emperor.

"Yes, sir, Mr. Edmonds?"

"I'd like to know exactly what in hell is going on here."

"Sir?"

"With Graves."

"He's just having kind of an off day."

"Need I remind you that we play Sterling the day after tomorrow?"

"No, sir, you certainly don't need to remind me."

"And need I remind you that I have a great deal of influence on who will and who will not be the manager of this baseball team?"

At this point, both Susan and Byron cast their eyes down and sat in rigid embarrassment as Clinton Edmonds got louder and angrier and as everyone within earshot began hearing him.

"No, sir, I guess you don't need to remind me. No, sir, you surely don't."

"Then you go talk to Graves and tell him I want to see at least five strikeouts in the next two innings."

"Yes, sir."

"And by God, I hope you're taking me seriously."

Harding gulped, nodded and then trotted back to his team.

Clinton Edmonds said, "I am surrounded by incompetents. Surrounded by them." He glared at Byron Fuller. "Aren't I right, Byron? Aren't I surrounded by incompetents?"

Byron looked miserably at Susan. It was obvious she did not want him to agree with her father.

But meekly, Byron said, "Yes, sir. You are surrounded by incompetents."

He knew he dare not look over at Susan.

T.Z. was still thinking about the girl in the tavern last night.

His tastes seemed to change. Constantly. One day he liked the type of sophisticated women he'd known in Chicago and St. Louis, other days he preferred the working girls of smaller towns.

To T.Z. women were power and he had understood that since an incident that took place when he was eight years old.

A nine-year-old, a bully who seemed to have a special dislike for T.Z., beat him up savagely in front of other children on the way home from school.

T.Z. had never been hit so many times or in so many places.

Finally, he fell on the ground, bleeding from eyes, mouth and even ears.

The others, including the bully, had run away, leaving him there in the chill autumn afternoon.

Despite the temperature, despite the fact that he knew he should get up and hobble home, he could find no strength for anything but lying there, letting the pain pound through him.

Then he'd felt a warm and gentle palm on his forehead, and when he opened his eyes, he saw a girl he knew to be in the grade ahead of his bending over him. He knew one other thing about her too. She was generally regarded to be the bully's girlfriend.

"I'm sorry he did this to you," she said, and he noticed there were tears in her eyes.

She lifted his head and poured water from a cup into his mouth.

"My name's Audrith," she said, as she then helped him to his feet.

Between swollen lips, T.Z. had said, "I'm T.Z."

"I know who you are. I mean I've—" He saw she was blushing. "I mean I've noticed you around before. You're—"

She stopped then, embarrassment claiming her completely.

Even through his pain he wanted to hear her say it because he saw the way she looked at him and he sensed in her glimpse real power for himself. Money he had not; nor the strength of even an average boy; nor was he especially intelligent at schoolwork.

"You didn't finish what you were going to say," T.Z. had said.

"Oh, it wasn't important."

"Of course it was." And he'd faced her directly. "Everything you think is important. To me, anyway."

So that afternoon, as purple dusk gathered, they took the long way home, down by the railroad yards, where the great trains linked and unlinked like huge metal dinosaurs copulating, and as they walked, and the more she blushed, he sensed within himself his growing power.

There was a crooked creek, silver with the season's first membrane of ice, and they stopped there and found cold water for his face. And once his face was clean, he did what he'd been longing to do, and what he knew she had been longing for him to do—he kissed her, right there and right on the lips.

And he was almost overwhelmed with his power.

Three more times the bully beat him before the snow flew, but from this experience T.Z. learned that he had one thing most men did not have and would never have—a real grip on the hearts of women.

Let the others boast of strength or gold; T.Z. had his looks and his laugh, and no matter how imposing the man, there was a good chance, if T.Z. applied himself, he could steal the man's woman—maybe for no more than an hour or two, but steal her nonetheless.

Lying on the bed, late summer sunlight rich red gold across his slender body, T.Z. sighed.

In the three months following the death of that baggage car man, there had been little time for women. There had been time only for running and hiding and jumping at even the vaguest hint that he and Neely had been discovered.

And that was why the nightmares were back. The one about holding the old man in his arms and crying for him not to close his eyes because when he did close his eyes, all history would come crashing down and there would be only darkness and oblivion and—

"Easy," Neely said.

"What?" T.Z. said.

"Easy. I said it was going to be easy."

Neely sat over in the corner of their hotel room. He had been at the table with his tablet and pencil for more than an hour.

Neely was always this way before any kind of operation, no matter how big or small.

Neely liked to draw diagrams in blunt pencil strokes, the way military commanders did before battles. Strategy, it was called.

"We hide in the closet and then, when the guard goes, all we have to do is sneak out and unlock the safe."

T.Z. smiled lazily. "I didn't know you knew a whole hell of a lot about safes."

"Don't need to."

"Then just how do you propose to get into the safe?"

Neely frowned. "Since when did you start worrying about how I handled things? I've always handled them all right in the past, haven't I?"

T.Z. sat up on the bed, lit up the yellowed remains of a quirly. "The kid's got things good here. I want to get that money without anybody finding out that he even knew us."

"I've got it all figured."

T.Z. kept his eye on him. "I'm serious, Neely. I don't want nobody to know that the kid's my brother or that he's got anything to do with us."

Neely stood up and smiled. "You don't sound real scary, pretty boy, when you make threats like that." He picked up T.Z.'s shirt from the chair and then tossed it to him. The smile was long gone. "Come on. We're going to go watch a little baseball."

Sullenly, and without a word, T.Z. put on his fancy lace shirt and his string tie, and then his fancy-cut black coat.

"I want you to go easy on the kid, Neely. And I'm serious," T.Z. said.

Neely just shook his head. "You're a pathetic bastard, T.Z. You know that? Whose idea was it to come to Cedar Rapids anyway?"

"Well—"

"Who said, 'My brother works in a bank. He can get us some money.' Was it me, T.Z.?"

"Well—"

Neely shook his head again. "Like I said, T.Z., you're one pathetic bastard. You know that?"

Then they went to the ballpark.

CHAPTER TWELVE

In the seventh inning, the sky vermilion and banked with golden clouds, Harding came out to the mound.

The score was 6–5. The second team was beating the first.

Les Graves stood slamming the ball into his glove. The cheers of the crowd had long ago vanished into the gathering dusk.

Harding, reaching him, said, "You gotta concentrate, Les."

Les looked up. There was a wildness in his eyes. "I am concentrating."

"No, you're not. Just before you throw, your eyes move to the right. To the stands."

Les sighed.

"I know who you're looking at."

Les shook his head, fearing the answer that Harding would offer.

"You're looking at Clinton Edmonds."

Les frowned. Harding was half right. He was probably, in fact, looking to the right, just to the west of the batter's box, but it was not Clinton Edmonds he was looking at. It was Susan Edmonds.

"You remember how I told you to relax?"

"Yes."

"Then try it."

"I—I don't know if I can."

"C'mon, Les. You gotta try."

"All right."

Les turned slightly away from the manager, closed his eyes and began taking a series of deep breaths and trying to blank his mind entirely. Harding insisted that an ancient Sioux Indian who lived up near Parnell had taught him this trick. (Les had never had the courage to ask Harding what an ancient Sioux Indian was doing up near Parnell, when the Sioux reservation was three hundred miles north.) But he tried it. He pictured in his mind his toes and then his legs and then his groin and then his stomach—all the way up his body to his brain itself—relaxing, relaxing, relaxing . . . and in truth, the tension did seem to flow out of his body as his awareness of the crowd, even Susan, began to diminish. His felt his muscles surrender, surrender . . .

A few minutes later, Harding said, "Now, we're going to do that again when we're up to bat and you have some more time. Now, you just step up to the mound again and everything's going to be fine."

Les smiled. "I sure hope you're right."

"You just wait and see. That damn Sioux chief I told you about knew half the secrets of the universe."

This time the ancient one was a chief. The last time his name was invoked, the man had been a mere warrior.

Les laughed. "You sure you knew this Indian?"

"You think I make up shit like that?"

"Hell, yes, I do."

This time Harding laughed. "You should be ashamed of yourself, Graves."

He walked back to his team, waddling a bit because not only was his stomach spreading as he reached forty but so was his backside.

Les, continuing his deep breathing, and concentrating, *concentrating,* stepped up to the mound, shook off two different signals from the catcher, waited till he found one he liked and then sailed one so fast and so fine across the plate that the crowd went flat-out crazy again.

He struck out the next two batters and trotted back to the home team side with the crowd giving him a standing ovation.

The fat man had himself two more soft drinks and then took the folded-up poster from inside his jacket.

It was a crisp folder, recently printed, and if you held it close enough to your nose, you could smell the printer's ink, which was one of the fat man's favorite odors in all the world.

He opened the folder and pressed it flat, and stared at the visage of T. Z. Graves and the big bold word WANTED and then that glorious figure $5000 DEAD OR ALIVE.

Only crazy people trifled with the railroads, which, in this year of Our Lord 1884, virtually if not literally owned the country. (It was said that in the halls of Congress, the paintings of George Washington and Thomas Jefferson had been replaced with the portraits of J. P. Morgan and James J. Hill.)

T. Z. Graves had not only robbed a train. He had killed a railroad employee.

Even desperadoes as popular and pampered as the James Brothers had paid for foolishness of that magnitude, Jesse shot dead just a year and a half ago, and Frank James going through a series of bitter trials that could yet end up in his hanging.

Just how did T. Z. Graves think he stood a chance against the might and cunning and tirelessness of the railroad?

The fat man had some more of the cool drink and watched as Les Graves ran back to the home team side.

The fat man smiled as his eyes followed Graves. That was one trick the railroad men, beginning way back when Allan Pinkerton was just a tyro, learned well.

You didn't stalk the criminal himself. You stalked his family. Because when you got the family, you got what Pinkerton liked to call "leverage." The fat man had heard Pinkerton give a talk in St. Louis once. Pinkerton said that the Romans had learned one truth about torture—that some men you can torture for hours, days and get nothing from them. But take these same people and threaten to torture somebody they love and—the men broke almost immediately.

The fat man leaned his arms back and enjoyed the sight of the teams trading places on the field and the men in their new straw hats and the women in their floral hats and the kids with pennants and homemade baseball caps made up to resemble those worn by the players.

You got to a man through his loved ones, the fat man thought contentedly to himself.

And that was just what he planned to do.

Neely said, "Remember the year the White Stockings won twenty games in a row?"

But T.Z. wasn't listening. T.Z. never listened when the subject was sports. T.Z. had his women and his nightmares and that was about it.

They stood at the north end of the bleachers, watching the game in its last inning.

"Boy, there sure are some pretty ones in this town," T.Z. said.

Neely said, "There are pretty ones everywhere."

"Yeah, Neely," T.Z. said, "but you never seem to do anything about it."

"Wasn't my fault she ran off with that goddamn drummer."

"You could always try to find another one."

"She'd be just like Myrna was."

"Myrna wasn't so bad."

"If she wasn't so bad, why did she run off with that goddamn drummer?"

"Maybe she got tired of your politics."

Neely shook his head. "I never understood that."

"Understood what?"

"Why she hated me talkin' about politics."

"Women don't give a damn about things like that."

"Some women do. Look at the suffragettes."

T.Z. laughed. "The suffragettes. Hell. Who gives a damn about them?"

But suddenly Neely wasn't paying so much attention to their argument. Suddenly Neely wasn't paying attention to anything but sight of a certain man way up high in the east section of bleachers.

There was a kid behind them in the stands with a pair of field glasses.

Neely leaned over and said, "Want to make a penny?"

"For what?" the kid said suspiciously.

"For your glasses?"

"You mean buy them?"

"Just use them."

"For how long?"

Neely wanted to crack the kid across the face. The kid was ten, chunky and mean-looking.

"For no more than a minute."

"What the hell are you doin'?" T.Z. asked Neely.

"Shut up," Neely said.

"A nickel," the kid said.

"All right," Neely agreed, tossing and flipping him a nickel. "Now give me the glasses."

"No more than a minute," the kid warned.

Neely jerked the glasses out of his hand.

"What the hell's going on?" T.Z. asked.

"I already told you," Neely said, as if to a child. "Shut up."

Then Neely turned the glasses east to the bleachers where he'd spotted the man.

He adjusted the glasses to get the best look possible.

The kid said, "It's been more than a minute, I'll bet."

T.Z. said, "You watch your mouth, kid."

"He promised," the kid said, sounding as if he were going to start crying. "He said a minute. One minute."

"Shut up," T.Z. said.

"Shit," Neely said, not taking the glasses from his eyes.

"What is it?" T.Z. asked.

"Shit," Neely said again.

Then he yanked the glasses from his eyes and plumped them back in the lap of the kid.

He started walking very fast for the exit from the ballpark.

T.Z. had to half run to keep up.

"What's wrong, Neely?"

But Neely didn't say anything more than "Just keep your head down and move as fast as you can."

T.Z. always got scared. He was scared now. "What's wrong, Neely? Tell me, please. What's wrong?"

"Like I said," Neely said through gritted teeth. "Keep your head down and move as fast as you can."

Thirty seconds later they had left the ballpark. That was when Neely broke into a full run and headed for the maze of the railroad yard down in the valley below.

T.Z., trying to keep up, said, "I'm scared, Neely. I'm real scared."

But all Neely could think about was the glimpse of the fat man in the bleachers and who the man was.

And why he'd be here in Cedar Rapids.

CHAPTER THIRTEEN

A home run won the game by a single run for the first team. The second team had never come this close to beating them before.

The crowd's applause was sparse.

Clinton Edmonds, all curses and bluster, got up and stalked from his box seat, Susan and Byron following meekly in his wake.

The fat man sat up in the bleachers until nearly everybody had left the park. Dusk was full in the sky now, a low and gorgeously purple dusk, with a scattering of bright stars and a full moon so vivid it looked like a painting.

The fat man made his way carefully down the bleachers and back to the Grand Hotel, over on Second Street East. He had a last glance at Les. He would see the man later tonight.

Harding, the team manager, went through his usual postgame talk, spiced with derision, occasional praise and finally a vaguely patriotic theme ("Our ancestors didn't come to this country so you men could look as rotten as you did today"), and then he dismissed the team, warning them not to drink more than one bucket per man at Pearly's tonight.

Les did not need to be told that Harding wanted to talk to him privately.

Les sat at the far end of the bench, elbows on hands, staring at the starry sky. So many things crowded his mind—Susan, T.Z., what a hanging would look like, the bank robbery plan Neely had outlined last night—so many things that it literally exhausted him to contemplate them.

Then an image of May Tolan came to him, the memory of her this afternoon in the hat shop. Her eyes and the look he'd imbued them with. Yet for all his guilt over May, thought of her gave him some comfort. He was thinking of her when Harding came up.

Instead of speaking, or standing over him as he usually did, Harding sat down next to Les, very tight, like kids on the front seat of a buckboard, and he didn't say anything for a long time, and when he did finally speak, it wasn't about baseball at all. He said, "Boy, don't you love the smell of dewy grass on a summer night?"

"It's great," Les said, sounding as if it were anything but great at all.

"And haven't you ever wondered just how many stars there are in the sky?" Harding said, sweeping his hand to the heavens as if he were a minister invoking his flock to passion for God's handiwork. "When I was a boy, my mother always let me sleep in the front yard and I'd always fall asleep counting the stars."

"I was terrible tonight," Les said.

Harding said, "You shouldn't think about that. You should just sit here and let this splendid night seep into your bones."

"We barely beat the second team. And it was my fault."

"Not entirely. Nobody played real good tonight. Not real good at all."

For a time Les said nothing. "I wish we had another pitcher."

"You're being crazy," Harding said. "And you're not telling me the truth."

"About what?"

"That's what you're not telling me. About what's bothering you."

"Nothing's bothering me. I'm just nervous about the game."

"Les, you've pitched for two seasons and never had any trouble at all. You're the best ball player I've had in ten years of managing. And now all of a sudden—"

Les sat there and looked at Harding in the fading light. Harding wanted some kind of explanation for Les's performance, so Les decided to give him one. At least a partial one.

Les told him about his experience trying out with Chicago a few seasons back. How he'd gone there a real hotshot and how for the two days preceding the actual start of training camp, he'd been fine, throwing every kind of pitch imaginable and throwing so fast and skillfully that even some of the pros had come over to watch him.

But then came the day when he put on the uniform and took to the field and felt the hardened professional gazes of the manager and the owner and then—

Then he tightened up and his fluid style became sluggish and strikes became balls and he beaned two batters and threw several pitches in the dirt and—

And then he was out of training camp.

Another yokel on his way back to Yokelville bearing the indelible mark of shame for being unable to make it as a real ball player—

"You got scared," Harding said gently.

"Yes. I guess that's what it was anyway."

"Scared was all."

"Well, whatever I got, it sure wasn't good."

"Scared."

He looked at Harding. "Maybe that's happening to me again."

"You don't have to let it."

"I don't know how I could stop it."

"You pray?"

"Sure I pray."

"Well, then go over to St. Patrick's and pray your ass off. I always pray to St. Joseph. My old man was a carpenter. I figure that gives me special privileges. So get over there right now and pray to St. Joseph and mention my name. You'll see a difference. I promise you."

Harding always made him feel better—he liked the man's simple and passionate belief in his own personal world and code—and he wanted to tell him about it all—Susan and T.Z. and how he was getting drawn into a robbery he wanted no part of.

But he couldn't, of course.

About Susan, Harding would simply say that he was playing out of his league and should find another game (Harding liked to put everything in sports terms) and about T.Z. and Neely, Harding would say go to the police. Harding was an honest workingman and he resented the easy way criminals elected to take. He would have no time for T.Z. and Neely, especially once he discovered they'd killed a man.

"That sounds like a good idea," Les said finally.

"St. Joseph?"

"Yes."

"Well, then go to it."

Les stood up, stretched his arms wide over his head. It felt good. "Well, at least we didn't get beaten tonight, anyway."

"That's right. You've got to think positive. And that's how I want you to be at noon tomorrow."

"What's noon tomorrow?"

"That's when Sterling gets here."

"But I thought the game was the day after tomorrow—"

"It's still on for the Fourth. But they've decided to get here a day early so they can practice for a couple of hours in our park."

"Well, I guess that isn't so bad."

"They're showboats," Harding said.

"What?"

"Showboats. Show-offs. They're going to have something special planned for us tomorrow, wait and see. Something meant to intimidate us."

"Like what?"

"I don't know. But that's their style. The time they played Minneapolis, they had their infield start singing every time a good batter got up to the plate."

"Singing?"

"You bet. You know how that would break a fella's concentration? You're standing up there and you've got the bat in your hand and you're one run down and you know you've got to swat it out of the park and the pitcher winds up and then suddenly the shortstop starts singing this song—"

"Singing!" Les was astounded and broke into real laughter. "Those bastards!"

"That they are, and more. They're real circus performers, you wait and see, and they'll do everything they can to intimidate you."

Harding threw an arm around Les. They walked down the length of the bench under the starry night, through the sweet and dewy grass.

"You go say some prayers to St. Joseph," Harding said.

"I will, Harding. Right now."

"Promise?"

"Promise."

"And why don't you skip Pearly's tonight."

"Don't worry. I will. I need some sleep."

Harding gave him a little squeeze and said, "You're a good man, Les. A damn good one."

Les nodded thanks and set off into the darkness, headed for St. Patrick's. Praying did not sound like a bad idea at all.

"Black Jake Early."

"The Pinkerton?"

"Used to be a Pinkerton. Now he's a free lance."

"Bounty hunter?"

Neely nodded. He had turned up the Rayo table lamp and closed the curtains. In the small hotel room were the commingled smells of kerosene and tobacco smoke and whiskey.

Neely said, "He must've gotten ahold of Dubbins."

"But how?" T.Z. still whined, childlike.

"Who know? All that matters is that he found out."

"He's going to come after us, isn't he?"

Neely took out the makings and began quietly rolling himself a cigarette. When things got very bad, this was how Neely got. Quiet. You could tell he was thinking and thinking deeply, but his hard Irish face gave you not a clue what he was thinking about.

Neely licked the cigarette and put it in his mouth and popped a stick match with his thumbnail. He waited till he'd taken the smoke heavy into his lungs and then he said, "I'm worried about Les."

"What about Les?" T.Z. sat on the edge of the bed. He had his hat on now. He took it off and put it on without seeming to notice. That was how T.Z. got when things got bad. He went straight to hell.

"You asked if Black Jake Early will come after us. He won't. First he'll go after Les."

"Why?"

"Good Pinkerton training." Neely exhaled bitter smoke. "I ought to know. I fought enough of the sons of bitches in my railroad days in Montana." He took another drag, parted the curtain, looked out at the gentle night. "They get your family involved and then they've got somebody they can use against you. If you know your mother or your sister or your wife is being intimidated by the Pinkertons, then you tend to stay around to protect them." He shrugged. "You stay around and they grab your ass. Every time."

T.Z. threw himself back on the bed. His fancy Texas hat went tumbling off. He resembled a seven-year-old who'd been told he couldn't go to a certain birthday party. "If we'd gotten here a week earlier we could already have the money and be headed for Mexico. Now we'll have to go without it."

"You're wrong, T.Z."

T.Z. sat up. "How the hell we going to get any money with this bounty hunter in town?"

"First of all, we don't know for absolute sure that he's here for us. Doubtful as it is, it could be some kind of strange coincidence. Second of all, the Mexes aren't real nice to gringos who don't have any money."

"But how—"

"We need to think it through. How we get the money *and* get rid of Black Jake Early."

"He's supposed to be good."

Neely shrugged again. "He's supposed to be mean, is what he's supposed to be. Mean isn't necessarily good."

"He's got my poster. You can bet on that."

Neely looked at him and thought: You're helping me, kid. You're making it easy for me. By the time I shoot you, I won't feel a damn thing about it. Not a damn thing at all.

Neely said, softly, "You get some sleep, T.Z. You know how you'll get otherwise. Nervous and all."

Neely stood up.

"Where you going?" T.Z. asked.

"He hasn't got my picture on that poster. Besides, there are things that need to be done."

"Such as what?"

"Such as I need to contact your brother. Tell him how to handle Early when he shows up."

T.Z. looked at him. "This Early, he kills people, doesn't he?"

Neely smiled humorlessly. "Like I said, T.Z., being mean doesn't make you good. If that was the case, every bullyboy drunk in every bullyboy tavern in America would be a tough guy." He put some humor in his smile finally. "Now, you be sure not to leave this room, all right? With Early around, we don't want to take any chances."

Good little boy—good little frightened boy—that he was, T.Z. said, "Don't worry, Neely. You just do what needs to be done and I'll be right here."

Neely put on his white Stetson with the brown leather band and said, "I'll see you later then, all right?"

"All right, Neely. All right."

Then T.Z. lay down and started staring at the ceiling and already his lips were moving.

He was praying.

The sight of pretty T.Z. lying there praying and on the verge of tears sickened Neely.

He got out of there.

To reach St. Patrick's, Les walked along the river, skirting the Czech part of the town. From a tavern he heard accordion music and as he neared a bakery he smelled kolaches filled with poppy seeds and strawberries and slices of apple. Of all the ethnic groups in Cedar Rapids, the Czechs were probably the best cooks, with fine dishes ranging from roast goose to liver dumpling soup.

When he reached First Avenue he saw a streetcar stopped for passengers and decided to board it. His uniform attracted enough attention from the elderly people aboard to embarrass him. The conductor getty-upped the horse and the streetcar pulled away.

The ride was twelve blocks.

On the corner of the church was a streetlight of the old sort. The lamplighter had been here already this evening. The stone church front looked steep, as if its cross were literally lost in the darkness above.

Inside, Les dipped his hand in the holy water and crossed himself. He stood for a moment in the vestibule, watching the way the green and yellow and blue and red votive candles played in the gloom surrounding the altar. The air smelled of faded incense.

He went up the wide aisle and genuflected and went in a pew where, without hesitation, he began praying. There were so many things wrong in his life. Nothing in Cedar Rapids had turned out to be as he'd hoped.

Back in Illinois four years ago, when he'd finally gotten courage enough to leave his brother and Neely behind, Les had had two dreams. One was to play professional baseball. The other was to become a respectable citizen.

He did not care if he carried a workingman's lunch bucket or if he ambled down the street in a fine business suit—as long as he was respectable. For he'd never known that as a boy. Because of his father's hidebound love for whiskey, they had lived in hovels, and even then they'd been turned out by landlords who drew solace from the misery of others.

To be respectable—that was the real reason he'd retreated here to Cedar Rapids.

And now—

So he prayed. He tried the Our Father and the Hail Mary but they were only words, words he could not quite feel. So he put his grief and fear and dreams into simpler and less fine words—and began to feel the relief and comfort that Harding had promised.

He was just about to go up and light a votive candle when the deep strains of a pipe organ startled him.

He turned around in the pew to look up into the choir loft.

And there, unbelievably, standing next to the organ, a hymnal in her hands, was the woman he'd longed all day to see.

May Tolan.

CHAPTER FOURTEEN

Susan sat on the veranda of her father's estate house, reading tonight's edition of the *Evening Gazette*. There was a breeze at last and the house was quiet. Her mother was knitting, her father upstairs in his den, doing paperwork.

She did her best to concentrate on the stories in the paper. She tried not to think of Byron and his impending visit ten minutes or so from now. She especially tried not to think of what she was going to tell him.

She had been on the veranda for the past hour, so she'd managed to get through nearly every line of the paper.

—There was the story titled A MIDNIGHT RAID: "The gambling den of McDonald's, one of the half dozen that grace the city, was raided with good success by the police last night. About 'the very witching time of night, when churchyards yawn and hell itself breathes out contagion to this world,' Night Chief McDaniels and four men forced an entrance into McDonald's den in the Southern hotel just in time to break up a very exciting game of 'draw' in which four or five well-known and highly respectable gamblers of the city were taking part." The story went on to detail the fines and sentences dispatched the men by Judge Leach.

—A man named Liddell was testifying in Huntsville, Missouri, against Frank James. The story noted that several times spectators hooted at some of Liddell's alleged "facts."

—Lillie Langtry was appearing for the next few nights at the Greene Opera House in her own company's production of W. S. Gilbert's *Pygmalion and Galatea*. (If Susan hadn't been planning what she'd been planning, she might have asked Byron to take her before Miss Langtry left town.)

—There was a shoe sale at Geo. A. Cobban's, with ladies' shoes for as little as $1.50.

—There was an editorial titled "The Kid Nuisance," which was

aimed angrily at dissuading parents from bringing infants to the
opera house and having the howling brats spoil everybody else's
evening.

—There had been a lynching in Magnolia, Miss., which described
how a Geo. Lee, "colored, age 18, was arrested yesterday for assaulting a child of four years and lodged in jail. Last night a mob of 100
men came from McComb, took Lee from the jail and hanged him."

—There was a story about immigrants in trains "of eighteen cars
each, who passed through Cedar Rapids en route to Dakota. They
came from Toronto, Canada, and were for the most part good,
healthy, honest-looking people who would thrive in any country."

Then there were the personal notes—a Miss Busbee was described
as "Queen of the Rollers" at the Roller Rink and how the ladies of the
First Baptist Church would give "a literary entertainment" a week
hence, for which admission would be fifteen cents; and then, as always among the personals, there were sad notes: "Frankie, son of
Mrs. Rosella Mumphrey, died Saturday, aged seven weeks and one
day"; and a Mrs. Sargent of the Southwest side was being placed in
the home for the insane.

She was starting to reread some of these stories when she heard a
rustling among the tall hedges that surrounded the veranda. Byron
knew the secret path.

He also seemed to know what she was about to say, because when
he came through the hedges, his eyes were downcast and his mouth
was a thin, grim line.

"Hello, Susan," he said, obviously trying to put some jauntiness
into his voice despite the dead quality of his gaze.

"Hello, Byron."

"I sure would appreciate a glass of lemonade. It's so hot."

From the pitcher on the table, she poured him some lemonade.
He sat in the chair next to her.

She said nothing for a time and he seemed to understand that he
dare not say anything, either.

She watched the moon, the vivid, mysterious, silver moon.

"Have you ever wondered about the moon?" she asked.

"Sure."

"If we'll ever get there, I mean."

"Sure," he said again. "I told you about the French writer named
Jules Verne."

She was silent again for a time and then she said, "I wonder if it will be more peaceful there."

He sighed, sensing where the conversation was heading.

"When I was a little girl I used to run up to my room and hide in my closet with a pillow over my head, just so I wouldn't have to hear my father yell at my mother and my brothers. But no matter how far back in the closet I went and no matter how tightly I pressed the pillow over my head, I could still hear him. And I always did the same thing. I'd shake so that I couldn't stop and then I'd begin to cry and I'd keep crying until I was literally exhausted. I lived under his tyranny all those years." She stared at the moon again. "Now it's time for me to leave home and start my own life."

"Susan, this afternoon—"

Her voice was little more than a whisper. "I don't blame you, Byron. I really don't. I love you for your gentleness. You're the most tender man I've ever known. But you're no match for him. No match at all, I'm afraid, and he would rule our lives just the way he did when I was a little girl. And I couldn't stand that anymore, Byron. I really couldn't."

She had started to cry.

He came to her, knelt before her and put his head in her lap. She stroked his head there in the moonlight and the rose-rich night.

"I love you so much, Susan."

"I know," she said. "I know."

"And I'm sorry I let him intimidate me." He raised his head and got to his feet. He began pacing the flagstone veranda. "I—I have these plans."

"Plans?"

"Yes. Plans to—to 'tell him off' as they say. To step right up and say, Clinton, you owe me some respect just as a fellow human being. At Dartmouth we had a philosophy professor who subscribed to that very theory. That every human being on this planet is entitled to respect just because he draws breath." He ceased his pacing and looked down at her. "Every morning of my life, just before I enter the bank, I make my plan. I think: The first time Clinton singles me or anybody else out for his wrath, I'm going to march right into his office and tell him—not disrespectfully but very forcefully—tell him that every human being who draws breath deserves respect."

"But how long have you been planning it?"

He sighed. "Years, I have to admit. Years."

"And you won't ever do it."

"I'll surprise you someday."

"I'm afraid you won't, Byron. That's what I'm really and truly afraid of."

After a pause, he said, "Lillie Langtry is at the opera house, you know."

She said it very simply, the way the most terrible things are often said. "I won't be seeing you anymore, Byron."

"My God, Susan, do you know what you've just said?"

"Yes."

"And you're serious?"

"Yes."

"But, Susan—"

"I may be going away."

"But where?"

"Maybe I'll go to live with my Aunt Juanita in Omaha."

"But Omaha—"

"It's a nice enough city. Progressive."

"But our plans—"

She could see he was in shock and she felt terrible for him.

But lately the griefs of her girlhood had begun to overwhelm her again. She needed a man who could protect her from her own father.

And Byron, much as she loved him, simply was not that man.

He stood over her now and took her hand.

"All I can ask is that you reconsider."

"Byron, I haven't come to this decision rashly."

"But I can change. You'll see."

"Byron, you've said that for so many years. I've asked you over and over again not to let him—" She sighed. "You know how he treats you."

Byron said, "Maybe I'm not the weakling you think I am."

"I don't think you're a weakling," she said softly.

But he seemed angry now, defensive. "But that's what you're saying, isn't it?"

"No, it's not, really. It's just—you let my father cow you."

"And I suppose Les Graves wouldn't?"

"Les Graves?" She wondered if he knew about the dozen meetings she'd had with Les.

"I saw the way you watched him the other night. Heard the admiration in your voice when you talked about him."

She shook her head. All Byron referred to was how she'd praised Les's pitching.

"I said he was a good athlete was all."

"But you seem to run out of any kind words for me. When was the last time you called me a 'good' anything?"

She saw how hurt he was and sensed that the conversation was about to turn pointlessly vicious.

She stood up and walked over to the edge of the veranda. She listened to the night's dogs and barn owls and birds.

"I'm sorry I've hurt you," she said, her back to him. "Maybe I'll change my mind once I've been in Omaha awhile."

"Omaha!" he scoffed. "I wish you'd get that damn silly notion out of your head!"

His voice had been like a rifle shot.

Her mother came to the French doors. "Are you all right, Susan?"

"Yes," Susan called back. "I'm fine, Mother."

"You're sure?"

"I'm sure."

"Why is Byron so upset?"

"We're just talking, Mother. It's all right. Really."

There was a pause and then her mother said, "Why don't you give Byron some lemonade?" She made it sound as if a simple glass of lemonade would make the world a completely better place to live.

After her mother had returned to the parlor and her knitting, Susan said, "I'm sorry I've hurt you, Byron."

"I'm sorry I got so angry."

"I understand."

"I hope you're not serious about Omaha."

"I think I'd like to give it a try."

"I—I'll miss you so much I'll be insane, Susan. I mean that."

"I'll miss you, too, Byron. You don't know how much."

Then suddenly he took her into his arms and said, "Then don't go. You don't have to go. I'll change. You'll see. I'll prove it to you."

Gently, she pushed him away. "I should go in now, Byron."

"But, Susan—"

"Please, Byron." She touched his fine face with her silken hand. "Please let's not hurt each other anymore. I really need to go in."

In the moonlight, his eyes were silver with tears. His voice was a rasp. "I love you, Susan," he said.

And then he turned and ran, vanished into the secret parting of the hedges.

She heard him run through the dewy grass and leap over the creek nearby and land heavily on the other side, and then keep on running through the night, as if the sheer energy of it would give him succor.

As perhaps it would.

Then she turned and went up to the French doors and stood looking for a time at her mother. What a splendid house. What a splendid prison.

Before her father broke her as he'd broken her mother and brothers, Susan would leave.

She went upstairs to write her aunt in Omaha.

There were seven hotels in Cedar Rapids, four of them in the downtown area.

Neely spent the next forty-five minutes going to each one trying to find out if Black Jake Early was staying there.

At each hotel Neely took from his pocket a fat leather wallet, pinned into the flap of which was a heavily ornamented four-pointed silver star.

"Yes, sir," the clerk at the final hotel said when he saw Neely's badge.

"There's a man I have some interest in."

"Interest in, sir?"

Neely paused, giving the man as sober a stare as possible. "Yes. An interest in."

"I see. An interest in." The way the man said it, Black Jake Early might have been guilty of anything from burning down orphanages to sedition.

"Now, I'm going to describe him and I'd like you to think very hard and see if he might not be staying in your fine hotel here."

When he said this, Neely glanced around the sad lobby, where several men gummed, a few of whom lacked various limbs, told and retold Civil War stories. The place stank from the meat-packing house five blocks away. Neely wondered if late at night, lying on their beds, they could hear the animals screaming as they were led down the ramps onto the killing floor.

The man still stared at Neely's badge. People's fixation on authority had always bothered him. Show a man a badge and his voice would take on the cowed and toadying cadence of a child seeking a favor. He lost all dignity. Even when he'd been part of the labor movement back in Chicago—even the socialists had set up a hierarchy with leaders and symbols little different from those of the government they wanted to tear down.

"I'll be willing to help any way I can, sir," the clerk said. He was skinny and wore a red string tie under the soiled collar of his white shirt.

Neely closed his plump wallet and put it back in his pocket.

"He's very big," Neely said. "Very big. And he usually wears a black Stetson and three-piece suits and he's got a small scar just to the left of his mouth—"

"Good Lord," the clerk said.

"Excuse me?"

"He's here. Right here at this hotel. Good Lord," the clerk said nervously, glancing around as if an invading army were camped just outside the plate glass window, which had been taped back together after some accident.

"He's in the hotel, then?"

"Well, not right at the precise, exact moment, no, sir."

"But he is staying here?"

"Oh, yes, he's staying here."

Neely leaned even closer to the man. "You didn't happen to talk to him, did you?"

"No, sir, he's just not that sort."

"What sort?"

"The sort you talk to. Not unless he talks to you first."

"I see."

"Have you ever seen him? Up close, I mean?"

"No, I guess I haven't."

"It's his eyes."

"What about them?"

"Well, sir, we've had our share of roughhouses come through here —this place doesn't always attract the genteel sort—but this man's eyes . . . They're mean. The kind you read about in the newspaper. When they talk about how killers look."

"Killers," Neely said, letting the man's imagination do all the rest. "Maybe now you know why it's sort of important we find this man."

Now it was the clerk who leaned forward to Neely. "What's going to happen? If there's going to be trouble, I'd better send somebody up to Mound Farm."

"Mound farm?"

"That's the part of town where the owner lives."

"There won't be any trouble. At least not right now. I just need you to help me out a little bit."

"Help you out how?"

Neely nodded to the room keys on the hooks behind the man. "I need to look in his room. Just to make sure he's the right man."

For the first time the clerk showed some hesitation. "Boy, sir, I don't know. I really think I'd better get the owner down here. It wouldn't take more than a few minutes."

Neely raised a skeptical eyebrow. "Just time enough for Early to come back and know that we're on his trail."

Then the clerk's frown changed to a half smile. "I guess I didn't think of that."

"I need that key. For just a few minutes is all."

The clerk scanned the lobby. As if somebody might be watching them or overhearing.

From outside on the hot air drifted the smells of freshly killed hogs.

In England some of the socialists Neely had met were vegetarians. He'd thought of being that himself, sometimes.

He put out a hand and the clerk put a key in it.

"You really got to be quick about it," the clerk said, an edge coming back into his voice.

"I'll be very quick," Neely said. "Very quick."

He went through the lobby and up the stairs and down a long hall smelling of cheap pine and bleach. The sounds coming from behind the doors put him in mind of the hospitals he'd been in at the end of the war. Coughing, spitting up, groaning— He'd had a leg injury but that wasn't half as bad as the noises he'd had to put up with during his three-week stay.

Early's room was at the end of the hall. He slipped the key into the lock and went in.

The place was what you expected. Shabby furnishings and a bed that sagged in the middle. You smelled sweat and you smelled piss. The window was open at least and there was a slight breeze.

In the corner Neely found a big, colorful carpetbag. He dumped it out on the bed, working in the dim illumination of the streetlight outside, going through its contents one by one. Shirts—two expensive white ones; trousers wide enough to fit two normal-size men inside; a book, *Kidnapped*, by Robert Louis Stevenson; rags and oil for cleaning guns; socks, underwear, string ties.

Then he found it.

A stiff piece of white paper folded in half.

He took it over to the window and opened it up so he could get a good look at it.

There was T.Z.'s image. The baggageman had lived just long enough to give the railroad authorities a very good description of T.Z.

Neely went over and put everything back inside the carpetbag.

So that's why Black Jake Early was here for sure.

For T.Z.

From inside his suit coat pocket, Neely took a pencil stub. He went over to the bureau and found a piece of paper, and then he quickly wrote a note. It said:

> YOU WANT T. Z. GRAVES. I WILL HELP YOU FIND HIM. I WILL CONTACT YOU TOMORROW NIGHT. I EXPECT A PART OF THE REWARD FOR THE RISK I'M TAKING.

He put the note right on the bed, right where Black Jake Early would be able to see it the moment he walked into the room.

Then he stood for a moment in the long shadows of the shabby hotel room.

He thought about what he'd just done. In the days when he'd had ideals left, he could not have even conceived of such a thing. But nothing meant anything anymore. He had seen too many starving and wounded children and too many murderous rich people to believe that the world made any sort of sense at all. You did what you did to prolong your life as long as you could—feed your hungry belly, find a roof to keep out the rain, take pleasures where you found them (liquor, furtive women)—and then you died and there was just oblivion and you left behind you starving and wounded children and murderous rich people.

So in the scheme of things, it did not really matter that he would betray T.Z.

There was just oblivion waiting and no, it did not matter at all.

But for all his hardness, he was shaking and sweating unduly, and he left the room abruptly, as if something in it had threatened to contaminate him.

CHAPTER FIFTEEN

She sang "Angus Dei" and "Oh Beautiful Mother" and then there was silence and Les just sat in that silence there in the church, afraid to make a move and afraid not to make a move, lest May Tolan leave the church before he had a chance to see her.

He heard the lid closing on the organ and then he heard the organist say "Good night, May" with a whispered clarity that echoed off the tall ceiling.

"Good night, Clarissa," May Tolan whispered back.

Then there were footsteps creaking down the choir loft stairs as the organist left and then the sound of the heavy front door being pushed open with some effort by a frail woman. For a moment there was the smell of apple blossoms from outside commingling with the incense in the church. The door fell shut again and once more there was just the silence.

For a time Les just stared at the altar ahead of him, at Christ crucified above the communion rail, cruel spikes through the palms of his hands and the arch of his crossed feet. The crown of thorns looked sharp from even this distance.

I want a respectable life, Les thought, and it was a prayer, this thought, a prayer that would allow him to transcend the bitter streets where he'd grown up and to forgive himself for the weak man he'd been in his early days, always going along with T.Z. and Neely no matter what they wanted to do.

I have not been a good man but I can be, he thought as his eyes rose again to Christ there on His cross.

And then he heard creaking footsteps on the choir loft steps.

May was leaving the church.

He crossed himself and genuflected and then got out of the pew and walked quickly down the wide, shadowy aisle to the gloom of the vestibule.

In the darkness he smelled her familiar, gentle perfume.

He saw the crack between the two front doors, a slice of gold moon revealed as she pushed one door open, and then his pace became a half run.

She was down the steps, hurrying, by the time he had passed through the door.

"May."

But she obviously pretended not to hear him, continued to hurry down First Avenue toward the small white house where she lived with her spinster aunt.

"May."

But she did not respond this time either. Simply kept her small feet moving.

All he could think of was her eyes this afternoon. The pain in them. The pain he'd *put* in them.

"May."

But his voice was lost this time to the leafy elms lining the street; the fireflies carried his sound off with them into the summer night.

He moved on instinct, knowing he would have no idea what to say once he actually caught up with her, but knowing he had to take some kind of action or go crazy.

So he trotted up to her and fell into step with her.

She had small, pretty features and in profile she always looked very young, like a pretty and sad girl whose face had not quite formed.

"Please just go on, Les," she said.

"I—I need to talk to you, May."

"Please, Les."

"I need to say I'm sorry if nothing else."

She stopped and looked at him. The same look that had been in her eyes this afternoon was there now. Behind her on the street an ancient horse plodded along pulling a wagon with a sleepy driver. From several blocks away you could hear the water rushing over the dam at F Avenue. She folded her hands in front of her, over her prayer book, looking prim in her high-collared yellow dress. May's sweet slender body always managed to make inexpensive cuts of cloth, which she made into dresses herself, look imposing. Her hat was a wide-brimmed straw affair with a clutch of roses set against the right side of the crown.

She said, and she said it softly but with a curious strength, "I know you're sorry, Les. That's the kind of man you are. You're sorry for half the things you've done in your life."

"I'm not going to see her anymore, May."

For just a moment he saw a fresh pain and even a hint of jealousy in her eyes, but then he watched as she consciously took hold of herself. "She comes in the store, you know."

"Susan Edmonds?"

"Yes."

He didn't know what to say.

"She's very beautiful," May said.

He still didn't know what to say.

"And you know what the worst thing is?"

"What?" Les said.

"She's very nice."

"You really mean that?"

"Yes. Yes, I do."

"Well, I guess she is. Nice."

"There are some young women from the better families— Well, they're not always so nice. But Susan Edmonds. She's—"

"—nice," Les finished for her.

"Yes—nice." It was obvious May didn't know what to say either. She looked at him a moment longer and then she began walking again, down the avenue fragrant with summer flowers and beautiful with a moon all the more golden for the fleecy clouds passing over it.

He stood and watched her retreat and then he caught up with her again.

"Susan and I aren't going to— Well, we're not going to see each other again."

"I'm sorry."

"Why are you sorry?"

"Well, I expect you feel the same way I did when you told me about Susan."

"I'll tell you the truth."

"And what would that be?" she said with just a trace of anger in her voice.

"I don't know what I feel."

"That's what you said to me four months ago, when you told me you were seeing Susan."

"I'm just—confused is all."

"Part of it is probably the pressure from the game."

"Maybe."

At the street corner, she paused and startled him by taking his hand. "Les, I still love you, but right now I can't help you. You're heartbroken and there's nothing I can do about it."

"I'm not sure it's that, May. I'm not sure I'm heartbroken. I think it's—a lot of things."

For the first time her gaze seemed to imply that she sensed trouble in him that went beyond Susan Edmonds.

"My brother's in town."

"Oh, God," May said. "And with that other man?"

"Neely? Yes."

During their time together, Les had told her many things about himself. He had not told her about helping with that one bank robbery, or about all the minor trouble he'd been in as a youth. But obviously she'd imagined some of the things left unsaid.

"What do they want?"

He sighed. "I wish I could tell you. I wish I could tell somebody."

She grabbed him by the elbow. "Don't give in to them, Les. He's your brother and I know how much you love him and how much you feel you owe him for helping to raise you—but don't destroy your life over him."

He exhaled raggedly. "I—I'm scared, May. I guess that's why I looked you up."

"Oh." The single syllable carried a tinge of disappointment.

"One of the reasons, I mean. May, I—" He shook his head. "If I said I missed you and that I still loved you, well—I couldn't be sure of why I was saying those things right now. You understand?"

"Yes. Yes, I understand."

"But I still think about you all the time and I think about all the things we used to do and the places we used to go and—"

She took his hand again. "Les, don't give in to them. Don't go along with them. Please."

"He's my brother."

"That's still no reason to—"

He blurted it out, unable to stop himself. "And he's in bad trouble, May. Very bad trouble."

Within the past twenty-four hours a certain image had come to play in Les's mind, one which just came alive with terrible vividness at odd moments. One over which he had no control at all.

He saw T.Z. being led up to the gallows. The hooded executioner. The dangling noose. The trapdoor being tried, so they'd know it worked for sure. And then the image always became T.Z.'s face. T.Z. would look the way he had the night their father died, T.Z. sobbing and screaming "Don't close your eyes! Don't close your eyes!"

Because T.Z. would know that he himself would be closing his own eyes. Soon and forever.

"You can't let yourself get dragged into—whatever it is," May said. The control she'd had over herself was going fast. "Promise me, Les. *Promise* me."

"I've got to help him."

"But he'll destroy you, Les, just the way he's destroyed himself."

"He's not bad—not inside."

"I can't judge him, Les. That's not my place. You were raised differently from me. We didn't have any money, but we did have a strong mother and father and that makes a difference. I know he's your brother and I know he's had a terrible life—but so have you, Les, and you haven't turned out like him." She clutched at his elbow again. "Oh, please, Les, promise me you won't let him talk you into anything."

He sighed. "All right, I promise."

She leaned away and looked at him.

"I'm afraid, now."

"It'll be all right."

"I don't care if I lose you to Susan. I could get over that. But if I lost you to prison or—something worse—" She shook her head.

He realized that she had begun to cry, and then she turned away from him and started walking the half block left to her aunt's place.

He started to catch up to her but this time she turned around and said, "I need to be alone right now, Les. I'm going to say some prayers for you. Because I'm so scared."

And he knew enough to let her go, her prim form disappearing into the darkness lying between the splash of streetlights.

He stood there for a time thinking mostly of T.Z. and what might happen, and then he thought of the coming baseball game.

How could he ever pitch it with all these other things on his mind?

He hurried on his way home to Time Check, hoping that tonight he could get some sleep.

After leaving the note for Black Jake Early, Neely left the hotel and started walking north out of Cedar Rapids, along the railroad tracks. He remembered a deep woods in the hills surrounding the town. He also remembered something else.

It took two hours to find what he was looking for.

He left the tracks and climbed a steep hill thick with underbrush and burrs that stuck to him like sucking animals.

Twenty feet back in the trees he saw the cabin. In the days when the railroads were laying rail from coast to coast, they occasionally built cabins for the supervisory crews that would stay behind. The buildings were sort of administrative outposts. But this late in the century, most of the cabins had been deserted, left to wild animals and the elements.

The doorknob had rusted and was stuck, so Neely had to kick the door in hard.

Then he went inside and stood amid the smells of mud and mildew, dog turds and a yellowing stack of newspapers.

There were three cots and a desk and a wall with hooks that had been used to hang clipped papers to.

He went over to one of the mattresses and sat down on it. Enough dust came up to make him sneeze.

He stood up. He picked up two of the mattresses and took them outside and began slamming them against a spruce tree. The night was alive with insects and the odors of ginseng and wild ginger.

Then he took the mattresses back inside and put them on the beds.

T.Z. would complain at first, of course.

T.Z. always complained.

He'd say it was dirty and that the prospect of mean dogs and snakes scared him.

He'd say he'd only stay out here if Neely stayed with him.

Neely took out the makings and had a cigarette. The moist tobacco taste was sweet in his mouth. He exhaled, watching the way the moonlight fragmented through the branches of a pine tree.

Since leaving the note in Black Jake Early's room, Neely had come to calmly accept what he was doing. T.Z. was wanted—admittedly for a crime that Neely himself had committed—and was known to the law and so their traveling years were over.

T.Z. was too dangerous to be with.

And anyway—and this was the most difficult of things to admit to himself—anyway he was tired of T.Z.

His nightmares.

His women.

His fears.

There had been a time when Neely felt almost paternal to T.Z., but no longer. Now Neely was more like his keeper and the role had become a burden . . .

He finished the cigarette and stamped it out in the earth.

But there was one more thing he needed from T.Z. The combination to the safe at Clinton Edmonds' bank. Only T.Z. could convince Les to get it for them . . .

Neely went in and looked around the cabin once more, at the moonlight tumbling through the hole in the roof and shining on a broken kerosene lantern. He walked back outside, took in a good, deep breath of piney air and then walked back to town.

Les was half a block from home when a huge man stepped from the shadows.

"Evening," the man said.

Les, shaken by the man's sudden appearance, said, "Evening."

"Beautiful night."

"Yes, yes it is."

Les looked around him. The lights were out in most of the houses. Distant down the block he could hear Mr. Waterhouse's voice telling more tales of Cedar Rapids.

"You're Les, aren't you?"

Instantly, Les knew something was wrong. "That's my name."

"I guess we need to have a little talk."

"About what."

"About your brother."

"How do you know I've even got a brother?"

"Oh, now, Les, don't start saying things like that. You know and I know that you've got a brother. And you know and I know that his name is T.Z. And you know and I know that he's wanted for train robbery and murder."

"I've got a brother named T.Z. But I don't know anything about him being wanted for train robbery and murder."

"There's a tavern down the block. Why don't we walk down there?"

"Don't think I'd care to."

"Hate like hell to have to talk at your boardinghouse. I mean, everybody you live with's likely to find out."

"They're friends of mine."

"Don't doubt that for a minute, Les. But you know it's a funny thing. When you've got a good friend and you think you know everything about him, but then you find out something secret—say something like his brother being a killer and a train robber—well, you start looking at that friend in a slightly different way. You may not even want to. You may even try to stop yourself from it. But you can't. Because when you know something about a person, your mind changes. That's just human nature."

Les thought a minute and said, in a sigh, "All right. Let's go down to the tavern."

Neely got the Rayo table lamp going and then went over and nudged T.Z., who slept hunched up like a baby.

"C'mon."

"Wha's wrong?" T.Z. said. He wasn't even awake yet and he was scared.

"We got to move. Fast."

"Why?"

"Because I found Black Jake Early's room."

"And what happened?"

"I found the poster."

"My poster?"

"Yes."

"Neely, what the hell am I going to do?"

"We got to move fast, T.Z. Damn fast."

"Where we going?"

"You just got to trust me, T.Z. You just got to trust me. Start packin' your things."

T.Z. was up and off the bed and packing.

Neely watched him and for just a moment he felt the guilt again.

T.Z. couldn't help it that he was the way he was—

But then Neely couldn't help it that the baggageman had lived long enough to identify T.Z.

"Hurry up," Neely said.

"God, Neely," T.Z. said. "I'm hurryin' as fast as I can."

He was one of those men who are surprisingly nimble despite massive weight. All the way to the tavern he kept easy pace with Les, and when a dog jumped out of the shadows and nearly knocked him over, he stepped effortlessly out of its way.

Business at the tavern had thinned out. Tomorrow was a workday. The place smelled of yeast and the free Swiss cheese placed on big plates at several places along the bar.

When Les and the fat man came in, the six customers turned to stare at them. Several smiled at Les and one made the remark "You should be home sleepin' for the game."

His voice carried admiration for Les.

"You're something of a celebrity," the fat man said after the bartender had brought them two mugs of beer, the heads of which he'd cut off with the edge of his hand.

"I guess."

"Guess, hell. Right now you're the most famous man in Cedar Rapids. And I hear you're very good, too. You ever thought of trying out for the pros?"

Les glared at him. "I don't think you brought me here to talk about baseball."

The fat man smiled. "I guess that's one of the drawbacks to my job. I try to be nice to people, but they don't seem willing to accept it."

"Just what is your job, anyway?"

"It goes by various names."

"Such as?"

"The most popular is bounty hunter. But when I worked for Judge Parker, he always told me to refer to myself as an 'auxiliary peace officer.' That sounds a lot more official, I guess."

"Judge Isaac Parker?"

"You've heard of him then?"

Les stared at the fat man. "I don't think I'd brag about the fact that I worked for a man like that."

Isaac C. Parker had once been a Missouri senator who, after being turned out of office, had been made a judge by President Grant. In

seventeen years the judge had personally seen to it that more than
one hundred sixty men had been hung. In addition to outlaws, he
enjoyed executing anybody who had anything to do with the labor
movement or what he invariably called "anarchy." His executioner,
an emaciated man with a flowing white biblical beard and the gaze of
a zealot, was named George Maledon, whom the newspapers called
"The Prince of Hangmen." To date, he had hung sixty men and shot
down four others.

"My name is Jake Early," the fat man said, putting forth his hand.
Les did not accept the handshake.

Early withdrew the gesture and smiled.

"I guess I wouldn't shake my hand if I were you, either. I mean,
given what I'm here to do."

"You're Black Jake Early," Les said.

"That's what they call me. Because my mama was a Blackfoot
Indian, I guess."

Only a slight red cast to the man's skin gave any indication of
Indian blood. Otherwise he might have been a successful merchant
with his expensive suit and massive gold pocket watch chain and clean
celluloid collar and deep red necktie and Vandyke beard. Only the
Smith and Wesson .44 he wore strapped to his waist betrayed his real
purpose.

Early said, "He's here, isn't he?"

"Who?"

Early smiled and nodded to the bar. "Like that fellow said, you
should be home sleeping. You don't have any time to be sitting here
playing cat-and-mouse with me." Early had some beer, wiped off the
foam with the back of his thick hand. "I seem to have developed a
reputation for being rough sometimes."

"You've developed a reputation for being a butcher."

"I'm trying to make a point here."

"Make it."

"When I get riled, or when I feel it's necessary, I pursue men
without much mercy. That I'll admit. But I always try to contact their
kinfolk first so that things don't have to get that way." He smiled. "It's
a matter of playing the odds, Mr. Graves. The fewer men I have to fire
on, the fewer men who have to fire back on me. I have a wife and two
children and one of those children is about to make me a grandfather.

I want to live long enough to see that grandchild. So I'd just as soon take your brother peaceably."

"I don't know where my brother is. I haven't seen him in two years."

Early smiled again. "Do you know a man named Dubbins?"

Les said, "Sort of. He's a friend of my brother's."

"Well, he's also serving time in Judge Parker's jurisdiction for assault and battery. The judge gave him twenty years."

"Why should I be interested in that?"

"Because the judge asked me to interview him. The judge asks me to do that to some of the prisoners, sometimes."

"That's a fine-sounding word. 'Interview.' "

"As I said, sometimes I pursue men without much mercy. That's also how I pursue the truth." He had some more beer and then pointed to the bartender for two more. Les had not touched his. "In the course of interviewing Mr. Dubbins, I learned a number of things. And one of the things I learned was that your brother and a man named Neely planned to come here to Cedar Rapids and look you up."

"Well, they must have changed their minds. They're not here."

The bartender set down two beers and put out his hand. Early set some coins in it.

"You don't seem to understand the situation here, Mr. Graves."

"I don't?"

"No, you don't."

"Then explain it to me."

Early leaned forward on his elbows. "If at the end of this conversation you haven't agreed to turn your brother over within twenty-four hours, then I'm going to find him myself."

Les just sat there and stared at the man. His ears rang and his stomach was painful with knots. He did not know what to say or do. All he knew was that this man meant to kill his brother and he had no idea how to stop him.

Les had his first sip of beer. He needed it to wet his mouth, which had dehydrated from fear. "Just say, for the sake of argument, T.Z. is here."

"All right, for the sake of argument, let's say that."

"You're saying you wouldn't shoot him."

"Not unless he forced me to."

"What would you do to him?"

"Take him back to Judge Parker."

Les sighed. There was no hope. Either way—if T.Z. resisted or if he allowed himself to be taken back to Missouri—he would die.

Les said, "Well, he isn't here."

Early laughed. He seemed genuinely amused. "Cat-and-mouse, Mr. Graves. I thought we both agreed we didn't have time for it."

"I haven't seen him for three years."

"A few minutes ago you said you hadn't seen him for two years."

Les stood up. He was sweating and trembling and he felt as if he were going to vomit.

He kept thinking of Judge Parker's executioner George Maledon and his zealot eyes and the fact that he boasted he wanted to "hang two hundred men before the Lord sees fit to take me."

"You're not being very intelligent," Early said after Les had stood up.

"He isn't in Cedar Rapids. You're wasting your time."

"The newspapers like to print accounts of the men I've killed."

"Or how about the man you stabbed in the forehead?"

"Simple necessity, Mr. Graves. That's all." He looked down at his thick hands and shook his head. "I've apprehended more than one hundred men and I've killed only twenty-three of them. I'd say that's a small number, given the type of men I pursue."

"He isn't here. He wouldn't have any reason to come here."

Early laughed again but not quite so heartily. "He'd have a very good reason to come here, Mr. Graves." He stared at Les for a long moment. "You work in a bank and your brother's a thief. You could help him get some escape money."

Then Early went back to staring at his hands. In a voice little more than a whisper, he said, "Good night, Mr. Graves."

Les left.

CHAPTER SIXTEEN

"Good night, dear," Byron Fuller's mother said, bending over to kiss him on the cheek.

"Good night, Mother."

When she pulled back from him, she said, "You've been acting queerly tonight, Byron."

"Have I, Mother?" He didn't look at her. Simply stared straight ahead.

"Quite queerly."

Mrs. Thaxton Fuller was a large woman given to bustled silk dresses that somehow managed to make her look formidable instead of feminine. Her husband had made one of the city's first fortunes by organizing an insurance company that worked exclusively with farmers in areas that the larger companies in Chicago and Kansas City and New York did not want to risk. But the risk had paid off, as was evident by the fact that this was the second-largest estate in Cedar Rapids, and that its sprawling living room contained not only a real electric light but such items as a Louis XVI gilt bronze and Chinese porcelain candelabra and rare English pewter porringers dating back to the 1400s and several original paintings by Vandyke. Mrs. Thaxton Fuller was a great world traveler, and a great world spender, and it was entirely too bad that Mr. Thaxton Fuller, who had made the money, had died at age thirty-five of pneumonia, six months after his son was born and a scant year and a half after the first time that his company had taken in more than three million dollars in premium revenues. So it had fallen to Mrs. Thaxton Fuller to protect both her husband's fortune and her son's upbringing, both of which she had done perhaps too well. She went to the insurance company once a month and fired one or two people on the theory that this would keep all the others in line, and much oftener than that she demanded from Byron subtle expressions of filial allegiance that could have unmanned General Sherman.

"It's Susan, isn't it?"

Byron looked up at her. "I'd rather not talk about it."

Mrs. Thaxton Fuller clucked. She was a past master of clucking. "She's too headstrong, Byron. I've told you that many times."

He frowned. "Mother, I've already told you. I don't want to talk about it."

His words came out angrily, a rebuke.

His mother's retort was no less angry. "It's this age we live in. The suffragettes and all the rest of it. They just confuse women about their place and the natural order of things. Women belong in the shadow of their men."

A curious smile lit Byron's eyes.

"Do you find something funny, Byron?"

"Yes."

"And just what would that be?"

"You, Mother. I find you funny."

He had never taken this tone with her. It was exhilarating.

He got up from the chair and walked over to the wide fireplace, above which hung a huge oil painting of his father. He kept his back to his mother, studied the portrait of the man above him. His father had been handsome, no doubt about that, but it was not unlike Byron's handsomeness. There was something melancholic in the gaze and something weak in the mouth.

"You owe your mother an apology, Byron."

But Byron seemed not to hear. "I suspect something, Mother."

"I am waiting for an apology, Byron."

He continued to stare at the portrait. "I suspect it was you who made his fortune for him."

"The apology, Byron."

"I suspect you were the real power, not Father."

She came up and turned him roughly about by the shoulder.

"Have you lost your senses? Do you know how you're speaking to me—your own mother?"

Calmly, Byron said, "Susan is moving to Omaha."

Mrs. Thaxton Fuller seemed unable to keep a glow of satisfaction from touching her lips. "I'm sorry to hear that. But there are other women your age in this city."

"Other women who are more likely to be intimidated by you—the way Susan isn't?"

"It's not only me she's disrespectful to." Mrs. Thaxton Fuller snapped. "It's her own father."

"Her father," Byron said in a soft but considered way, "is a bully and a tyrant."

"Byron! He's one of the most important and respected men in this town!"

That was Mrs. Thaxton Fuller's only measure for judging a man's worth. His importance. True, she often expressed feelings that this or that man was a boor or uneducated or that he was not "cultural," but none of these failings mattered much if he was "important," meaning of course that his fortune was equal to if not more substantial than her own.

"He's destroying Susan and he's destroying me," Byron said. "I'm going to resign tomorrow."

"What!"

"And I'm moving out of the house."

"My God, Byron, you go over and sit down right there and right now. I'm going to get you a snifter of brandy and we're going to talk."

But Byron stood unmoving. "I'm going to talk to somebody about a job with the electrical company. That's the coming thing and I want to be a part of it."

But Mrs. Thaxton Fuller wasn't listening. She had crossed the room to pour from a diamond-faceted blue glass bottle with colored decorations of birds some of the brandy she had imported from a monastery in Italy.

"Here," she said to Byron, handing it to him.

She led him, against his will, to the walnut-framed armchair with the buttoned back, one of her favorites.

Once he was seated, his eyes still peculiar, still *most* peculiar, she handed him the brandy.

"Now, Byron, I want you to tell me what's troubling you."

"Susan is troubling me. I love her. I'm losing her."

"As I said, there are other women."

"I don't want other women."

Mrs. Thaxton Fuller sighed. "Then we'll see to it that you get Susan back."

He glanced up. "*We'll* see to it. You and I? She's not an acquisition, Mother."

"That isn't what I meant."

"Of course it's what you meant." He looked down at his brandy and shook his head. "I don't blame her for breaking it off."

"You don't?"

His eyes raised to meet hers. "No, Mother, I don't. I—I haven't been the man she needs."

"Don't be ridiculous."

"In fact, I haven't been a man at all."

"You've been to Dartmouth. You're the youngest bank vice president in the state. What are you talking about?"

He laughed. "I'm not sure we have the same criteria for manliness, Mother."

"So you're going to quit your job and move out of the house?"

"Yes, Mother, I am."

For the first time in many years, he saw tears in his mother's eyes. He was moved, of course, and sorry for her, for her particular type of loneliness and her need to dominate all people and situations—but he was also determined.

He was not going to back down.

He set his brandy on the small table next to the chair and stood up. By now his mother had begun to sob rather dryly, as if she did not quite know how, and Byron took her with great tenderness in his arms and held her, and the mere act of it was enough that his mother felt the freedom to cry.

"I love you, Mother, and I'll see you every Sunday and I'll get a telephone and you can telephone me anytime you like, but it's time I move out. It really is."

And then his mother startled him by pulling back her tear-red face. She laughed a peculiar laugh, a *most* peculiar laugh, and said, "I was afraid you were never going to move out, Byron. And it frightened me. I don't want you to be one of those men who live with their mothers. But—"

"But what?"

"But it had to be your own idea."

From her sleeve she took a handkerchief. She blew her nose. She looked up at the portrait of her husband. "Thaxton was like that. You said I was the real power behind your father. I wasn't. All I could do was plant suggestions—and let him come to the idea in his own good time."

He smiled at her. For one of the few times he could ever recall, he not only loved his mother, but in this moment he *liked* her as well.

She said, "I can go with you and help you find a decent place to live."

Now it was his turn to laugh. He slid his arm around her tenderly and said, "No, Mother, if I'm finally going to strike out on my own, I don't think it's a good idea to have my mother pick out my lodgings."

She smiled. "No, Byron, I guess that wouldn't be a good idea, would it?"

"You see fewer and fewer of them every year," Mr. Waterhouse said.

As Les reached the porch of his boardinghouse, he smelled the mint used in sun tea, and the lazy smoke of a cigar.

His mind still filled with images of his brother hanging, and the curiously detached attitude of Black Jake Early with him yet, he decided to sit on the porch with the other boarders and listen to the preacherly tones of Mr. Waterhouse and his tales.

"Fewer and fewer," Mr. Waterhouse said.

"Where have they gone?"

"Some of them have died off, I suppose," Mr. Waterhouse said. "Living on a reservation likely kills some types of people, I imagine."

So the talk was of Indians. It often was.

"I can remember seeing them," Mr. Waterhouse went on. "They'd camp outside of town and work the maple trees for sugar and then you'd see them traveling through Cedar Rapids on the way back to their reservation, bringing the sugar with them. There was a small army of them and sometimes they sang and sometimes they chanted and sometimes they laughed at us in just the same way we talked about them. Indian sugar, though, that was the sweetest sugar I ever tasted."

Then there was talk about sugar and cakes and how good certain kinds of desserts tasted on Christmas day and how nobody seemed to like fruitcakes much.

It was not the sort of dialogue that could take Les's mind from his problems.

So he sat and watched how the elms formed a canopy over the road and how the shadows from the streetlights seemed to chase themselves like silhouetted dogs down the center of the sandy street.

Then Mr. Waterhouse said a startling thing indeed. "The McIntosh boy got out of Fort Madison today."

Fort Madison was the state prison.

"The McIntosh boy? Who's that?" one of the boarders asked.

"David McIntosh? You really don't know who he is?" Mr. Waterhouse said. The way he asked it, you could tell he was eager to tell everybody.

"Nope."

"Well, I guess that isn't surprising."

"What isn't surprising?"

"Why you wouldn't know."

"Wouldn't know what?" the boarder asked.

This was how Mr. Waterhouse liked to tell his tales. Sort of tease you with them. You kind of had to force them out of him. He loved that.

There was wind. The summer leaves were so thick they sounded like waves of the ocean as the breeze trapped them and swung them first this way and then that way. A collie trotted down the middle of the sandy road looking tired, as if he'd been out chasing rabbits for the past few hours.

And Mr. Waterhouse, leaning forward now and taking a preparatory drink of his ice tea with the mint leaves floating in it, said:

"David McIntosh was the boy who lost a bank."

"Who lost a bank?"

"That's right."

"Now how could a thing like that be?"

"I take it you want me to tell you."

"We sure do," said the boarder.

Mr. Waterhouse had a bit more tea and then he said, "It's very simple, really. Back when Cedar Rapids only had one bank, David McIntosh was a farm boy who fell on hard times and came into town one day to rob that bank. Well, he stuck it up all right but he lost it."

"That's the part I don't get. How could he lose it?"

"Well, he got the money, all right, you see—a big leather satchel of it—but on the way out of town he stopped at a rowdy roadsider for some beers. That was one of the McIntosh boy's most terrible problems. His liking for beer. Couldn't leave it alone. That was why he fell on hard times in the first place."

"I still don't see—"

"I'm coming to that," said Mr. Waterhouse, heading off the impatience of his audience. "Well, a fellow who's just robbed a bank isn't about to walk into a roadsider carrying a satchel full of money now, is he?"

"Not likely."

"So you know what he did?"

"What?"

"He did what any right-thinking bank robber would do."

"What?"

"He buried it."

"Well, that sounds sensible enough."

"Yes, it does, till you stop to consider that because of his liking for beer, he had terrible blackouts."

"You mean he couldn't remember things?"

"Exactly."

"So what happened?"

"Well, he went into this roadsider expecting to have just a few mugs, but he couldn't quit with just a few, the McIntosh boy."

"So then what happened?"

"Well, he also had one other failing."

"What was that?" another boarder asked.

"He was a braggart. A terrible braggart. According to him there wasn't a man in the valley who could spit as far, slug as hard or womanize as long."

"But how did that get him in trouble?"

"Well," said Mr. Waterhouse, "imagine yourself a young buck of twenty-three or less with a penchant for drinking beer and a tongue that just loves to brag."

"So?"

"Well, then imagine that you've just stuck up a bank and gotten clean away with it."

"Well, I'll be damned," the boarder said. "Excuse me, ladies."

"He started bragging."

At this point the boarders, as if having just been told a joke, started laughing there in the splendid darkness of the July night.

"He started bragging to the people in the tavern that he'd just robbed the bank and that he'd gotten away with it," Mr. Waterhouse said.

"They probably got the sheriff."

"They certainly did. He came right out to the roadsider and took the McIntosh boy to what passed for a jail in those days and manacled him to a bedpost and then let him sleep off his drunk."

"But I still don't understand—" the boarder began.

"You still don't understand how he lost the bank?"

"That's right."

"Well, when he woke up in the morning and the sheriff came in and asked him if he'd robbed the bank, the McIntosh boy confessed right away. But then the sheriff asked him where the money was."

"My Lord," said one of the lady boarders, who was now anticipating what Mr. Waterhouse was about to say.

"And that was how he lost the bank—he couldn't remember where he'd buried the money," Mr. Waterhouse said.

"Did they ever find it?"

"Never," said Mr. Waterhouse with great and abiding satisfaction.

"You mean to this day?"

"I mean to this day."

"The money's still buried—"

"—somewhere," finished Mr. Waterhouse. "Somewhere."

"My Lord," said the same lady boarder who had said "My Lord" before.

So then everybody fell to talking about how now that the McIntosh boy was released from prison he'd probably start hunting his money again, even though (as Mr. Waterhouse went on to elaborate) literally dozens of men had searched for dozens of days and had never found that money at all.

The story made Les smile and he sat there and played with the absurdity of the tale the way he might suck on a piece of candy, slowly, savoring it.

For a lingering, luxurious moment he was filled with an overwhelming optimism that somehow everything was going to be all right— T.Z. and Neely would make it to Mexico without having to rob the bank where Les worked, and Black Jake Early would go back to St. Louis and give up his guns and live out his days playing with his grandchild.

But then, as if sobering up from a very happy drunk, he saw Neely's face, the cynicism and sadness and irony of that shanty-Irish face, and knew there could be no such ending for T.Z. or Neely—or for Les himself.

Because he loved his brother, Les was inextricably bound up in their fate, in the events that Neely was now setting in motion.

The return of his gloom exhausted him completely.

He stood up on shaky legs and said, "Good night, everybody."

"Wondered when our town's baseball pitcher was going to hie off to bed," said Mr. Waterhouse with affectionate irony.

"Well, now's the time," Les said.

"Good night," everybody said to him.

Somebody had been in his room.

Black Jake Early stood three steps over the threshold, his weapon drawn, sniffing and listening with the intensity of an animal alerted suddenly to danger.

Somebody had been in his hotel room.

Through the window the lamplight from below tinted the air with a thin yellow color, just enough so that Early could see only places for anybody to be.

He went to the bed and rather than get on his knees and look under, he simply picked it up and flung it aside.

Nobody was under it.

Then he went to the closet and stood to the right of it and jerked the door full open.

He waited a full minute, his massive body greasy with summer sweat now, and then stepped into the darkness of the closet, his eyes adjusting fully to the gloom, and looked around.

Nothing.

He started to check his bag on the bed and that was when he saw the note.

He picked it up quickly and read it:

> YOU WANT T. Z. GRAVES. I WILL HELP YOU FIND HIM. I WILL CONTACT YOU TOMORROW NIGHT. I EXPECT A PART OF THE REWARD FOR THE RISK I'M TAKING.

He read it a few more times, as if it might hold some secret code, and then he went over and sat on the window ledge and took out a big stogie and bit off the end and spat it on the floor. He spent the next few minutes just rolling the stogie around in his lips. Enjoying the tart sweetness of the tobacco leaves.

Who knew he was in Cedar Rapids to find T. Z. Graves other than

Graves' brother and obviously this note had not come from Les Graves? And how had somebody gotten into his room? By picking the lock?

He lit the stogie and then went and lit the table lamp. Then he went to the door and started looking closely at the lock mechanism. He looked for the type of scratches you invariably get when you jimmy a lock with any instrument other than a key.

He found nothing.

They had come into his room with a key. That was for sure.

He carried the lamp back to the table and turned it off and then he went downstairs to the desk.

"Somebody was in my room," he said to the clerk.

The frightened look in the clerk's eyes told Black Jake Early all he needed to know.

"I wonder if you would step with me into the manager's office, sir?" Black Jake Early said.

"The manager," the clerk, a terrible edge in his voice, asserted, "he's gone home."

"I realize that. But we need to talk in private."

"I—I just couldn't do that."

"Very well," Black Jake Early said.

He pretended to leave, but then he turned abruptly and went around the desk.

He grabbed the clerk and threw him to the floor. Black Jake Early knew many tricks. He relied now on a primitive one that was generally effective. While his body weight kept the clerk pinned to the floor, he took his thumb and hooked it up into one of the clerk's eyes.

"Have you ever seen somebody take out an eyeball?" Black Jake Early said. He was sweating more than ever and he was red-faced from the exertion, but he sounded calm.

"Please, please don't."

"It's a frail orb," Early said. "Now if I were to dig in just a bit deeper—" Which is exactly what he did, of course. He was not bluffing. He had dug out many eyeballs. The people always got hysterical on you and you couldn't get anything out of them for a time—they were literally berserk—but when you finally got them quieted down again, they invariably told you what you wanted.

Early gave his thumb a little twist. He could feel the eyeball begin to detach from the retina.

The clerk screamed.

"Now," Black Jake Early said, "I want you to tell me who was in my room and why you gave him my key. Do you understand?"

The clerk understood.

Only too, too well.

CHAPTER SEVENTEEN

George Buss said, "You going over to the depot to see them?"

Les, who had been distracted all morning, scarcely heard his friend. "Uh—what, George?"

"I asked, were you going on your dinner hour to see the Sterling team come in."

"Oh. Yes. Well."

George scrutinized Les carefully. "You didn't get much sleep again last night, did you?"

"Not a lot." There was a peevishness in his voice. Les always got that way after a few days of not sleeping well.

"You going to be all right to pitch tomorrow?"

"I'm going to be just fine!" Les snapped.

Several of the customers in the bank lobby looked up at the harshness of his tone.

Les, blushing, put his head down.

For his part, George just kind of frowned and continued to stare at Les with paternal concern.

Mrs. Fuller stood in the doorway of Byron's bedroom and said, "Do you know what time it is?"

Byron nodded at the big clock on his nightstand. "I know exactly what time it is, Mother. It is 10:37 A.M. on Wednesday, July 3, 1884."

His mother did not smile at his humor. "You're still in bed."

Tousled of hair, wrinkled of pajamas, Byron sat up and said, "Yes, Mother, that does seem to be the case."

"You should have been at the bank at eight o'clock."

"Well, obviously, I'd say I'm going to be all right."

She started into the room, her hand out, palm flat.

Byron put up a halting hand of his own. "Don't feel my forehead for a fever, Mother. I feel fine. Perfectly fine."

She stopped a few feet from his bed. The room was splashed with golden sunlight that made the mahogany furnishings look even darker and richer. His red-and-white flowered bedclothes shone brilliant in the light. The room smelled pleasantly of furniture oil. The maid had been in yesterday.

"It will not look good on your record."

"What won't look good on my record, Mother?" Byron said patiently.

"Why, being late, of course."

"Have you forgotten what I told you last night?"

"You were upset."

"I'm still upset."

"I would hope that you've changed your mind. You could be president of the bank when Clinton retires. And that won't be many years from now."

"As I told you last night, Mother, I'm going to resign."

She stared at him and made her familiar clucking sound. "So that's what this is about?"

"That's exactly what this is about. Why should I worry about getting there on time when all I'm going to do is go in and resign?"

Pity and then anger filled her gaze. "She's made you half insane, hasn't she?"

"If you mean Susan, no. Actually, she's helped me come to my senses. I hate the bank and I hate Clinton Edmonds. I'm wasting my life."

She came over and sat her formidable body on the edge of the bed. "As I said last night, there are other women. Many other women. Even if Susan moves to Omaha—"

He threw back the sheet that was covering him and said, "I really should be getting along, Mother."

"You're not listening to me."

"No, Mother," he said with barely concealed relish. "No, I am not. Now, please, let me get ready for the day, all right? It's a very important day. I'm going to apply for a position at the electrical company. Then I'm going to go look for new quarters, Mother."

Twice within the past twelve hours, he had seen his mother, a woman not given to the shilly-shally of tears, begin to cry.

It was not a sight he relished.

He leaned over and kissed her gently on the cheek and said, "You'll get used to it and so will I. It's time I grow up, Mother. It really is."

She gazed at him with something like panic now. "I need to ask you a question," she said soberly.

"What question?" he said, a playful affection having returned to his voice.

"You hear so much about—well, opium. You're not taking—"

He took her in his arms and bussed her on the forehead and said, "Really, Mother, can you imagine an upstanding Republican Presbyterian like myself taking opium? Can you really?"

And then she was crying and laughing at the same time and falling into his arms for support.

Neely had served ninety days in jail once for smashing the windows of a bank that was foreclosing on a sawmill that employed more than sixty people. He had learned, during that three-month stay, to sleep sitting straight up on the floor. This way the slightest movement, whether from somebody who wanted your body to carve up or to use as a woman substitute, either way you were ready for him, especially if your back was flat to the wall. You could spring up and disarm him with not much problem at all.

Neely, who had to grant Black Jake Early his prowess, had slept this way in the cabin during the night, flush against the wall just inside the door, his Navy Colt at his left side, his hunting knife at his right. T.Z. had slept on the couch. He'd had nightmares again—"Don't close your eyes!"—and Neely hadn't been able to take it this time, couldn't abide much of T.Z. at all anymore, so he'd gotten up and kicked him hard right in the ribs.

Now T.Z. stood over him, holding his side where Neely's shoe had collided with his bones.

T.Z. said, "You didn't mind killing that baggageman, did you?"

Neely had been thinking about his plan to bring Black Jake Early and T.Z. together tonight. His body was sore from the floor. He wanted to get up and smash T.Z.'s face. But then he didn't want to alarm T.Z. unduly, either. He wanted the Early-T.Z. meeting to come off tonight.

"What're you talking about, T.Z.?"

"I saw your face when you were hitting him. You were enjoying it."

"Hell."

T.Z. grimaced from the pain in his ribs. "You're supposed to be the great socialist, fighting for the common man. But you killed that baggageman and he wasn't anything more than just another working-man. And you enjoyed it."

Neely smiled. "You forget, T.Z."

"What?"

"My principles. I lost them a few years back. I'm not a socialist anymore. I'm just one more animal trying to keep his belly fed and his head free of all the lies the capitalists want to fill it with."

"You're a capitalist."

Neely was genuinely curious. "What the hell're you talking about?"

"You're a capitalist and so am I. We rob people, just the way the capitalists do, and we keep it all to ourselves."

Neely had to laugh. Occasionally T.Z. came up with a good one and this sure was a good one. "I shouldn't have kicked you so hard."

"You sonofabitch." T.Z. sounded as if he was going to cry.

So they stood a moment as dust motes tumbled in the sunlight coming gold and jagged down through the rough holes in the roof. Stood and stared at each other, two men who'd known each other since they'd been young boys playing guns with sticks and praying at the same communion rail. The air smelled of pine and heat, hard July heat.

"When we get to Mexico," T.Z. said, "I'm gonna go my way and you're gonna go your way."

"You sure you can handle it yourself?"

"You don't think I'm much better than a girl, do you, Neely?"

Neely laughed. "Truth to tell, T.Z., no, I don't." He looked at the man standing across from him. "One thing I've never been able to figure out is why women are so attracted to the men who are most like them."

"Just 'cause I don't like to fight doesn't mean I'm not a man, Neely."

"Who saved you in Canada?"

"I could've whipped him if he hadn't had a knife."

"And who saved you in Texas?"

"He got the drop on me is all. Blind luck."

"And who saved you in Illinois?"

T.Z. said, "I'm gonna do fine, Neely. I'm gonna do just fine." Then he made a face again from the pain.

Neely got up from the floor, brushed off the back of his clothes. "I'm going into town. See Les. We need that combination."

Anxiously, T.Z. said, "What if he can't get it?"

Neely smirked. "Then his brother just may hang."

"I'll go with you."

"Oh yeah, T.Z., you're gonna be fine when you go off on your own."

"What's that supposed to mean?"

"Black Jake Early's walking around Cedar Rapids with a poster of you in his pocket and so what do you want to do? Walk around Cedar Rapids, too."

"Cedar Rapids is a big place."

"Not that big."

"So you're just gonna leave me here?"

Neely looked at him a long time and then he said, "T.Z., when you're down in Juarez or wherever you settle, you going to telegraph me every time you need to make a decision?"

"You just get the hell out of here, Neely. I'm goddamn sick and tired of you."

"You clean your gun lately?"

"Huh?"

"Your gun. You clean it lately?"

T.Z. flushed, a guilty little kid. "None of your damn business." Which meant, of course, he hadn't.

"Well, I'd clean it and I'd keep it ready because that bastard Early is around and who knows that he didn't track you out here?"

Neely had to suppress a smile. T.Z. reacted instantly just the way Neely knew he would.

T.Z. got scared.

"You really think he'd come out here?"

"I wouldn't keep any more than a fingerful of air between me and the handle of your Colt," Neely said.

He went over to the door. He stood in the tumbling gold molecules streaming through the roof. "You'll be all right?"

"Why the hell you have to go into town, anyway?" T.Z. said.

Oh yeah, he was scared and wasn't Neely having a good time watching him.

"I'll be back in a few hours," Neely said. "Then I'll tell how we're going to kill Black Jake Early."

Then he opened the creaking door and went out into the piney woods and followed the fragile gait of a doe all the way to the sandy road leading east to Cedar Rapids.

Les was waiting on Mrs. Pike, a somewhat forgetful widow who liked to take her time with her banking, when May Tolan came in.

"Now, Les, let me see," Mrs. Pike said from the other side of the teller cage. "Did you give me my deposit ticket?"

"Yes, I did," Les said, indicating the yellow stub that she held in her right hand.

He nodded to the stub.

"Well, now isn't that funny," Mrs. Pike said. "It's right there in my hand."

Les smiled.

Mrs. Pike, satisfied, nodded and said, "I'm praying for you and the whole baseball team."

Les heard what she was saying but his eyes were on May, who still stood over by the front door, her purse clutched tightly in her small hands, her trim body arched anxiously inside its white summer dress. She wore, as if advertising for the store where she worked, an angled straw hat with a wide brim and a spray of blue artificial flowers.

Les was surprised at how happy he was to see her—and how nervous. He was afraid that she'd bolt like some skittish animal right out the door before he got a chance to talk to her.

Mrs. Pike said, "This is foolish of me, Les, but you did give me my safety deposit key back, too, didn't you?"

"Yes, yes I did, Mrs. Pike," Les said, an edge of irritation moving into his voice. Then he looked down at the farm woman and flushed. He liked Mrs. Pike. "I appreciate your prayers for us."

She smiled, pleased. "Well, you can bet I'm going to keep right on saying a lot more."

"Thank you, Mrs. Pike."

The widow nodded, looked at her deposit stub once more, as if it might have walked away from her since the last time she'd peeked, and then moved away from the teller window.

Les was left without a customer.

May stood watching him.

A businessman who had been filling out his stub started toward Les's window and Les felt instant disappointment.

But then May surprised him by moving quickly and reaching Les's window before the businessman did.

"Hello, Les."

"Hello, May."

Then neither of them said anything at all.

"I—I was glad to see you last night," Les said.

She set her violet eyes at an angle that did not quite meet his. "I was glad to see you, too." Then, almost in a whisper, she said, "Are you going to see the train on your lunch hour?"

"The Sterling team?"

"Yes."

He laughed. "A part of me's afraid to. They're supposed to be pretty scary to look at. Big."

Softly, she said, "I thought I might."

"Go see the train?"

She nodded.

He swallowed. "I could walk by your shop in a half hour or so and we could go over to the depot together."

This time her eyes did meet his. "I'd like that, Les."

"Me, too."

She clutched her tiny white purse to her breast once more. "In a half hour, then?"

He smiled. "I'll probably even be there a little early."

He was about to add something about maybe buying her some yellow roses, a display of which he'd seen down the street this morning, when he saw Byron Fuller come through the front door.

Les had been so concerned with his own problems this morning that he hadn't realized that Byron hadn't come into work until just now.

But that wasn't the only remarkable fact about Byron this humid July morning.

No, even more noteworthy was the fact that he wore a jacket and an open shirt with no tie at all, and in his hand rode a large hand-carved pipe. Clinton Edmonds had strict orders about bank employees smoking anywhere on bank property.

There was one other thing—Byron's eyes. Les couldn't tell if the man looked just plain happy or even a little bit crazy—or both.

May followed his eyes. "Is everything all right?"

Les shrugged. "I don't know."

"He's a nice man, isn't he?"

"Yes," Les said, "yes, he is."

Something about Byron's demeanor disturbed Les, only adding to the tightness he felt in his chest.

"Half hour," May said.

He brought his eyes back to hers. "I just realized a few minutes ago how much I've missed you."

The sadness was back in her gaze. "I guess my trouble was I haven't been able to forget how much I've missed you." Her knuckles were white against her white purse. "I'm afraid, Les."

"I've learned some things, May. I really have."

The door slamming behind him might have been the blast from a shotgun.

Everybody in the bank turned to stare.

"I'd better get back," May said.

Les nodded and smiled good-bye.

He watched May leave the bank, recalling so many good times they'd shared, and then his attention went back to the door that had just slammed.

Clinton Edmonds' door.

Only Edmonds hadn't been the one to slam it.

Byron Fuller had.

"Just what the hell do you think you're doing?" Clinton Edmonds demanded when Byron Fuller burst into his office and literally hurled the door back against its frame. Two sepia-tinted photographs, one of President Arthur, the other of Clinton Edmonds himself, tilted to the side from the force of Byron's entrance.

Clinton held a fountain pen poised above the ledger he was working on.

Clinton said, "And just what the hell do you mean coming in here three hours late without a tie and smoking a pipe?"

Byron said, "Put your fountain pen down."

"What?" Nobody had spoken in such a tone to Clinton Edmonds in longer than thirty years.

"I said, put your fountain pen down. I want you to hear every damn word I'm going to say to you."

"Have you gone crazy?"

"No, sir," Byron said, swelling his chest and exhaling pipe smoke like a dragon, "I've gone sane."

And with that he ripped the fountain pen from Clinton Edmonds' hand and proceeded to tell the man what he thought of him.

Neely stank by the time he reached town.

He found a small wooden shack where you could have a bath for 15 cents and a shave and haircut for the same amount.

Finished with that, he went over to a store named E. P. Van Valkenburg's and bought himself a new shirt for $1.10 and new trousers for $3.20. He changed right there and threw his old clothes away. He was in a celebratory mood.

Then he went looking for a place where he could set up the meeting tonight between Black Jake Early and T.Z.

A visitor to the city could easily tell that tomorrow was the Fourth of July. Flags flew from what seemed every possible angle and red-white-and-blue bunting seemed to envelop the entire town. In Greene Square, in the center of the business district, workmen were setting up a big bandstand and speaker's platform for tomorrow's ceremonies.

Neely had to go three blocks north of the business district, up by where water poured over a dam and smelled of fish. From here you could see an ice refrigeration plant where slabs of ice were swathed in straw and sawdust and blankets so they would not melt during the summer heat. Even though this was right in town, there was an open area where anything could happen and not necessarily be seen. Neely had found his place.

He decided to go have a beer before he hunted up Les Graves and got the combination. He had three beers instead.

"Have you ever seen Susan's hands twitch?"

"Just what the hell are you driving at?"

"I am," Byron Fuller said, "telling you that you've ruined the lives of your wife, your two sons and that you're doing your best to ruin the life of your daughter. And that I damn well won't let you ruin her life, Clinton! I won't!"

By now, Byron punctuated several of his points by slamming his fist on Edmonds' desk.

"Her hands twitch, Clinton—you know what I'm talking about."

"She has a nervous condition."

"Yes, and you're the cause of that condition."

Edmonds came up from his chair suddenly and just as suddenly his hand arced through the air and caught Byron on the cheek.

The slap sounded worse than it felt.

"I don't take this kind of insolence from any man," Edmonds said.

Touching his cheek, Byron said, "It's time you face the truth, Clinton. You're a miserable bastard who can't quit feeling sorry for himself that he was born poor—and you've spent your whole life taking that out on everybody around you."

"I'd say being born poor is better than being raised a pampered mama's boy, wouldn't you, Byron?"

Edmonds' slap had not raised color on Byron's face but his words did.

"I'm well aware that I've got some growing up to do," Byron said. "But I'm not the issue here. You are."

"My family is my own business."

"Not when Susan is involved."

Edmonds looked at him sharply. "Do you think I don't know what's going on? That I don't know what happened between you and Susan? She's going to Omaha next week. And she's called off her plans to marry you."

But Byron was getting angry again. "Do you know that a part of her really hates you, Clinton?"

For a shocked moment, Edmonds' face registered pain. "You're a damn liar. My children know that I occasionally have fits of temper, but they certainly don't hate me."

"Don't they, Clinton?"

"You'll get the hell out of here. Permanently."

"I need to clear out my desk."

Edmonds' face was red with fury and mottled with age. He looked ancient and forlorn. "You do that some other time, Byron. Right now I want to see you walk out that front door."

The ecstatic mood of his high, pure anger was gone now. Byron supposed he appeared just as depleted as Clinton. "I just want to say one more thing."

"I don't want to hear it."

"You don't have to be miserable, Clinton. Nobody gives a damn about your upbringing."

"Just get out of here, Byron."

Byron stood by the door a moment and then he said, "I still love Susan. I'm going to try to talk her out of leaving."

But Edmonds seemed lost now in his own torments. He wasn't listening. He had turned inward and sadness had replaced his bluster. Seeing Edmonds—the blustering, swaggering Edmonds—melancholy was almost frightening.

For all the anger he'd brought in here, Byron now felt at least subtly ashamed of himself. Perhaps there had been other ways to handle this— To tell a man that his own family hated him—

"Clinton," Byron said, "I shouldn't have said—"

Then Edmonds' temper returned. "Don't be a pansy, Byron. If you came in here to call me a sonofabitch, then call me a sonofabitch and don't apologize." He flung a hand toward the door. "Now get out of here."

Byron started to say something more—but what more was there to say—and then he left.

Quickly.

CHAPTER EIGHTEEN

You could hear the train carrying the Sterling baseball team coming half a mile away and it wasn't just the usual sounds of the train engine, either.

There was a band on board that train and it played as festively as if it were New Year's Eve.

More than four hundred people encircled the small frame structure of the Cedar Rapids depot, looking down the long shining stretch of tracks.

There were a lot of questions these spectators wanted answered. Was the average size of the Sterling player really six foot three and one hundred and eighty pounds? Did their pitcher, Fitzsimmons, really possess the operatic voice Sterling sportswriters always wrote of as "charming the birds from their nests in pure ecstasy?" Did the Sterling manager, Mike ("Mad Mike") McGee, really keep a small firearm tucked inside his belt in case an umpire made an exceptionally bad call?

You could not help but want to know the answers and that was why so many had turned out today.

To see a team that had come to possess, in the common mind, the glow of legend.

The train pulled into the station with the band playing "Camptown Races" in so boisterous a fashion your toes could not help tapping in time.

On the way over to the depot, May had slipped her arm through Les's.

They stood now, still arm in arm, toward the back of the crowd, where most of the Cedar Rapids baseball team could be found.

"They've got a pretty good band," J. J. Deamer, the center fielder, said. He said it with a certain note of suspicion in his voice, as if the music revealed something about Sterling's baseball prowess.

Elmer Novak, the second baseman, clapped Les on the back and said, "Yes, but they don't have our Les."

"You really think Mad Mike McGee actually carries a gun?" asked young Moray Uridel, the shortstop.

Novak laughed. "Don't worry, Moray. Harding's going to let us carry knives."

Then the train arrived.

The noise from the band, coupled with the squeaking metal brakes, was deafening.

The Cedar Rapids people got their first glimpse of the Sterling team through the clouds of steam rising from the train. The effect only enhanced the air of legend, as if the team were descending through the very clouds of heaven itself.

The first thing you had to notice was that the team wore uniforms. You'd think that on a hot, one-hundred-and-twenty-five-mile trip the team would want to wear their summer clothing instead of the woolen uniforms.

But they stepped down from the train in white uniforms with red trim and red caps with white trim (as if they had no life other than being a legendary baseball team), most of them with handlebar mustaches, all of them brushing at least six foot one or six foot two, and at least a fourth of them with noses that looked as if their off-hours were spent in fisticuffs.

They fanned out along the wooden platform in the way an army might have, just before assaulting an opponent.

The mayor of Cedar Rapids, a man with white hair and the manner of a tremulous minister, went up to the man everybody recognized as Mad Mike McGee and put out his hand.

A photographer, who had been nervously waiting for this moment, began waving them closer together for a picture.

Mad Mike McGee aimed a brown stream of tobacco juice about a quarter inch away from the photographer's foot.

Mad Mike, the only squat member of the Sterling team, looked as if he ate railroad spikes for breakfast. He had scars and he had tattoos and he had a prominent chipped tooth. Probably from eating railroad spikes.

"So this is Cedar Rapids," he said. "Never been here before. Never wanted to be, either."

The Sterling team roared.

The mayor, who was not a demonstrative man, said, "Oh, it's not such a bad place, Mad Mike."

"Hell, tell him where to get off!" somebody shouted from the Cedar Rapids crowd.

The mayor, realizing he'd just let down the citizens who had voted him into office, cleared his throat, and said, "In fact, it's not a bad place *at all,*" as if his words rang with courage.

Several in the Cedar Rapids crowd shook their heads at the mayor.

"Where's this Graves I've heard so much about?" McGee said. "Rusty Fitzsimmons wants to meet him."

When Les heard his name mentioned, his stomach began doing terrible things.

"Les? Is Les Graves here?" the mayor called, sounding like an usher paging somebody in the balcony of the Greene Opera House.

May, obviously seeing that Les was nervous, squeezed his arm and said, "You'll be fine, Les."

Les swallowed. "I hope."

"Les? Is Les Graves here?" the mayor continued to call.

"Right here, Mayor," Harding called back.

To Les, Harding said, "Now don't take no guff from that bastard."

Les wondered if Harding was referring to the mayor, Mad Mike McGee or Fitzsimmons.

Les sort of waved his hand so that the mayor could see him and then he sort of put a smile on his face and then he sort of went up to the head of the crowd. His stomach was twice as bad as it had been and he knew anytime now it would be three times as bad.

When he finally got a first look at Fitzsimmons, Les saw why all the sportswriters wrote about the man as if he was on loan from Olympus.

Fitzsimmons stood at least six two and had shoulders you could comfortably rest a boxcar on. He had a shanty-Irish face, which meant he managed to look both innocent and mean at the same time, and he had a smile he must have practiced as often as he did his fast ball.

"This is Graves?" Mad Mike McGee said.

"This," the mayor said, missing Mad Mike's disparaging tone completely, "is Lester Graves."

"God, Mayor," Les said, like a small boy who'd just been embarrassed by a parent, "you know how much I hate Lester."

"So it's 'Lester,' is it?" said Rusty Fitzsimmons, laughing. "That's an awfully nice name, 'Lester' is."

Even from ten feet away, you could hear Harding say, "Boy, that mayor's a stupid bastard."

"Well, 'Lester,' I'm Rusty Fitzsimmons."

And with that he put out a right hand whose palm was so big you could hide a baseball in it.

Les watched as his own, much smaller, hand traversed the empty space separating the two men and connected with Fitzsimmons'.

The pain was instant.

Never before in his life had Les felt a grip like this.

The ache started in his fingers and ran the length of his arm and even began radiating into his shoulder.

Fitzsimmons knew what he was doing, of course, and so his smile rivaled the sun's for sheer brilliance.

And he didn't let go, either.

Les wriggled his hand as much as he could without looking as if he was trying to wrench it free, but Fitzsimmons kept holding on.

"Quite a grip he's got there, don't you think, 'Lester?'" said Mad Mike McGee.

By now Harding had pushed his way up to the front of the crowd. The burly fireman said, "That's his pitching hand and you know it, Fitzsimmons."

Les felt hot blood start up his neck and fill his cheeks.

He felt a total fool.

"Well, so it is," Fitzsimmons said. "Now I sure wouldn't want to damage 'Lester's' pitching hand now, would I?"

"Let him go."

"Please, Harding, I can take care of myself," Les said. He was beginning to feel a lot like somebody who should actually be named Lester.

Later on, the newspaper account of what followed would accuse Harding, who had never been known for his even temper, of throwing the first punch. And so it was.

Harding took two steps toward Fitzsimmons, got just enough leverage to let go a short cracking hook to the jaw and fired.

If nothing else, Fitzsimmons let go of Les's hand. Right away.

But almost simultaneously, Fitzsimmons also decked Harding. With a single punch.

And that's when the general melee broke out.

The Cedar Rapids depot was transformed from a somewhat sleepy wooden platform filled with respectable men in celluloid collars and women in flowery summer hats to the scene of an all-out brawl.

The men of both teams managed to push the ladies aside and go at each other with a fervor the heat of the day only increased.

If you were not tall enough to crack a man on the jaw, then it was eminently permissible to kick him sharply on the shins (if not other bodily parts), and if you saw a friend of yours in trouble, then you were to forget all about Queensberry and come up from behind the man assaulting your friend and let him have a good and sinking punch to the spine.

Les was aware of throwing six (or maybe seven) punches at men in white uniforms and even more aware of taking twenty or so in return.

Given the fact that his nose was bleeding and that one of his front teeth was loose, he was not unhappy when a policeman stood up on a nearby baggage wagon and exploded a Smith and Wesson for attention and order.

The gunshot got everybody's attention immediately.

The few men who continued to swing were yanked to order by their friends.

The policeman, a well-respected Czech named Severa, said, "Say something, Mayor."

The mayor, standing on the ground, looked miserably up at Severa and said, "Why don't you handle it? You're doing a good job."

Severa frowned and shook his head and then barked to the men before him, "You're supposed to save your spunk for the playing field."

There was, of course, grumbling and cursing and various accusations as to who had started it. Severa raised his weapon as if to fire again. It was enough to bring back order.

"Now, I want one of you businessmen to help the Sterling team find their hotel," Severa said, "and I want the Cedar Rapids team to go back to their jobs or their homes." He paused. "Now does everybody understand me?"

Like chastened children—Severa was a thickset, impressive man—they all paid him at least the lip service of dutiful nods.

"Now," Severa said, "go!"

And so they went.

"Hurt?"

"Sort of."

"I'm being as easy as I can."

"I know and I appreciate it."

"How's your hand?"

"All right, I guess."

They were in Greene Square Park, Les and May, and she was seeing to his cut lip with cotton and iodine.

Les stretched his fingers out before him. Between getting them squeezed by Rusty Fitzsimmons and bruised by pounding them on people's faces, they were pained but seemed otherwise all right.

"Now let's look at that tooth," May said.

She put a tender finger to his loose tooth. "Boy," she said. "Boy, it's really loose."

He touched his tongue to it. "It's like when you were six and you had a tooth that was about to fall out and you kept on worrying it with your tongue."

She smiled at him. "I guess you're going to live."

"I guess I am."

She laughed. "And I guess that's pretty good news."

"Well, I'm happy to hear it, anyway."

So they sat back against the tree. The grass was very green and there were butterflies, some orange, some white, one even bluish, and there was a breeze that blew the tops of fluffy dandelions into a million pieces that floated on the soft currents of summer air.

She said, "I'm scared."

"What?" He was genuinely surprised by her remark. They had been sitting here so peacefully—he had even managed to quit thinking about T.Z. for a time—and now she was talking about being scared.

"I'm scared."

"Of what?"

"You. Me. Us."

"May, I—"

"I'm just going to ask you one thing."

"What?"

"This time don't make me any promises."

"But, May, I—"

"That's all I want you to promise me. That you won't promise me anything."

He was silent for a time, feeling how her thin body was tense against his. He sighed. "All right, May. I promise not to make any promises."

She stared straight ahead. "Thank you. We'll just let whatever happens, happen."

"Is it all right if I tell you how nice it is to be with you again?"

She turned and stared at him and then she smiled. "Yes, I guess that's all right."

And then a voice said, "Lovely day, isn't it?"

Les followed May's gaze to the right of the elm against which they sat.

Neely stood there. He was clean-shaved and wore new clothes. Even so, you could smell the beer on his breath and see the crackling anger in his eyes.

Neely doffed his hat. "I'm a friend of Les's," he said to May.

May looked at Les. Obviously she sensed his tension.

Neely said, "We need to talk, Les."

Finally, Les found his voice. "Maybe you'd better go, May."

"Are you sure?"

His throat felt constricted. "Yes," he said in barely a whisper.

He helped her up. They paused a moment, their eyes meeting. He gave her arm a tiny squeeze. "Why don't you come over to practice after work?"

"All right," she said.

She watched Neely for a long moment, as if he were of a species she had never seen before, and then she went on her quiet way.

"Pretty," Neely said. "Very pretty."

Les said nothing.

Neely pointed at Les's mouth. "Heard about the fight. That's going to be some game tomorrow. Too bad I won't be around to see it."

Les said, "I didn't get the combination."

Neely had a way of narrowing his eyes. You felt them like sharp little knives, cutting you.

"I take it," Neely said, "a man named Black Jake Early has contacted you."

Les stiffened, betraying the truth.

"I also take it," Neely went on, "that you know who he works for."

Les's mouth stiffened.

"I've heard that Judge Parker has a quota system he uses." Neely's voice was prickly with irony. "He can't sleep unless he hangs at least one man a month."

"I can't get it, Neely," Les said.

Some shopgirls went by and waved to Les. He waved back. They went on across the railroad tracks, seeming to float in their frilly summer dresses.

"He's going to get him, Les. Black Jake Early, I mean. He never misses."

Les put his head down, sighed.

"He's your brother."

Les, in a voice hoarse with grief, said, "I can't help him any more."

Neely let the silence grow between them. Then he said, "You're afraid of losing your life here, aren't you?"

Les looked up suddenly. "Yes—yes, I am, Neely, and I'm damn well not ashamed of it."

"Nobody would have to know."

"Of course they would know. I work in the bank."

"I've got that figured out."

Les shook his head. "I can't help you, Neely."

"It isn't me you're not helping, Les. It's your brother."

"You sonofabitch."

Neely laughed. "You never did like me, did you, Les, even when we were little kids?"

"All you did was manipulate people, Neely, pretend you wanted to help them. But the only person you've ever helped is yourself."

For the first time today, Neely lost his considerable temper. "Do you think it's been goddamn easy carrying your brother around all these years—he's drunk half the time and the other half he's running around with somebody else's wife and nearly getting himself killed. I'm the one who has to get him out of his scrapes. Not you. I'm the one who's taken care of him all these years."

Halfway through Neely's harsh words, Les began watching the other man carefully. He had never realized until this moment Neely's feelings for T.Z. Neely spoke with hard contempt. Neely hated T.Z.

Then Les felt a strange guilt.

Maybe Neely had earned the right to hate T.Z. Could Les have put up with his brother all these years? Could Les have endured his drunkenness and his nightmares and his dangerous womanizing?

T.Z., Les realized, was probably alive today only because hard, sober Neely had taken care of him.

Les sighed.

Neely, obviously sensing some shift in the other man, said, "Mexico will be good for T.Z. There's a clinic down there. This priest who's supposed to be good at sobering people up. That's where I'm going to take him."

"They'll find out," Les said.

"I'll make sure they never connect you with it, Les, I promise."

Les's eyes raised to fix on downtown Cedar Rapids. In the past two years this place had become his home. He liked standing on the corner of Third Street, right in front of the Guaranty Bank Building, and watching people stroll from the sunlight into the shade beneath the bright-striped awnings on the shops, then stroll out into the light again. There was the clang of the trolley and the sweet smell of heat on the oiled, sandy roadway.

Neely said, "Les, they'll hang him otherwise. They really will."

And all Les could do was shift his gaze to Neely and nod sadly in agreement.

CHAPTER NINETEEN

Just as Susan's mother finished telling her daughter what had happened at the bank this morning, there was a bold knock at the front door.

Susan and her mother were in the kitchen with its smells of potato salad and chicken being prepared for dinner on the veranda tonight. Mid-afternoon sunlight streamed through the mullioned windows. Jays and robins and wrens had collected on one of the bird feeders in the vast back yard. Their song imposed itself on the sudden silence in the kitchen as the two women waited to find out who was at the door.

Moira, the maid, appeared moments after the knock. "It's Mr. Fuller, miss."

Susan and her mother glanced at each other. "Is Father still upstairs?"

Her mother, who had been crying for most of the past two hours, nodded and promptly began tearing up again. "He's locked himself in his den. He won't come out."

"Then I'd best see Byron outdoors, in case Father should come down."

"I don't want him in my house, anyway."

Susan let Moira leave then. Despite her mother's teariness, Susan let her anger show. "You're not being fair to Byron, Mother. Father has treated him terribly all his life—just the way he's treated us."

"You should not talk about your own father that way."

"When I've seen Byron, I plan to go up and see Father."

Mrs. Edmonds looked past the lacy handkerchief she had pressed to her fleshy cheeks. "He's too hurt to let you in. In thirty-five years, I've never seen your father this way. So—despondent."

"He needed to be told."

Mrs. Edmonds flared. "Did he need to be told that harshly?" Her thin voice had risen to a scream.

Susan stood up from her chair. "I'm going to see Byron now, Mother. I'll be back soon."

She had turned to leave the kitchen, then paused and went over to her mother. She took the smaller woman in her arms and held her, rocking her gently, as if Susan were the mother.

Then she went to see Byron.

In the late afternoon, Neely still not back yet, T.Z. left the cabin, taking his pint bottle of rye with him, and went up in the bluffs that stretched to the north.

After Neely had left this morning, T.Z. had slept off the remains of last night's drunk.

He'd awakened pretty sober, given all he'd had to drink, and faced the one thing he hadn't wanted to face.

What he was doing to his younger brother's life.

He hoped to lose in the beauty of nature the dread and guilt that had been with him on waking.

He spent an hour in the bluffs, drinking all the time. At one point he came to the edge of a steep red-clay cliff and looked down on a railroad trestle that stretched over a sparkling expanse of clear blue river. A train wound its way westward, smoke beautiful against the sky. T.Z. wanted to be on that train, headed out to California, a state he'd always meant to see but somehow had never gotten to.

Would Les go to prison?

That thought cut through his entire time in the bluffs, ensured that he would have no peace.

He roamed a mile of sawtimber and wildflowers as various as bloodroot and wild ginger and ginseng; he saw pheasant and fox and squirrel.

And still the thought was with him: Would the bank officials tie Les to the robbery and—would Les go to prison?

He had more to drink and returned to the cabin.

Neely, in new clothes, sat outside the cabin door smoking a cigarette. A bluish haze partially concealed his angry gaze.

"Already, huh?" Neely said, nodding to the now empty pint bottle.

T.Z. resented his tone. He smashed the bottle against a rock. "Maybe I goddamn needed it."

Neely said, "Seems you're always needing it."

Then T.Z. surprised them both by saying, "I don't want to go through with it, Neely."

For the first time he could ever recall, T.Z. saw something like shock register on Neely's face.

"You don't want to go through with the robbery, you mean?"

"That's just what I mean. Just goddamn *exactly* what I mean."

T.Z. had these moods, a drunkard's bravery and honor. It was as if through the long and endless days of his drinking he would see what he had become, then try suddenly to deny his worst suspicions by doing something right and honorable.

"We've used the kid long enough. He shouldn't have to pay for what we did."

"Mexico's a mean place without money, T.Z. A damn mean place." Neely ground out his cigarette in the grass. "Anyway, I just got finished talking to Les and he wants to help us."

"Wants," T.Z. snapped. "He no more 'wants' to help us than anything. What you mean is, he's forced to help us because you showed him that WANTED poster and because he's afraid I'll hang."

Neely smiled coldly. "You know who he saw last night?"

"Who?"

Neely was obviously enjoying this. He knew how T.Z. would react to the name. "Black Jake Early."

T.Z. felt some of his resolve lessen almost immediately. His mouth got dry. Without a word, he plunged back into the cabin for another pint bottle. He came back out a few minutes later, wiping his mouth with the back of his hand. He needed a shave and a bath. Now the bird song that had lulled him for a time this afternoon only irritated him. "I want a good hotel room," he said. "I want a woman." He was getting drunk, fast.

Neely just watched him.

T.Z. wandered around in little circles, taking small drinks from the bottle.

He was thinking of his father now—of how his father had closed his eyes there at the last—and how that had been, at least, peaceful.

But hanging would not be peaceful.

No.

There would be the sneer of the mob and the cut of the rope and the drop of the trapdoor.

The panic was on him, then, and Neely seemed to be smiling

contentedly now and T.Z. knew just what Neely was thinking—that T.Z. was always easiest to handle when the panic was on him.

"He's my own brother, and I'm ruining his life," T.Z. said.

Neely just kept looking at him.

And smiling all the more as T.Z.'s resolve got drunk out and paced out and scared out of him.

"He's my own brother," T.Z. said.

But he spoke in a whisper and between drinks now.

"My own brother," T.Z. said.

The afternoon was a fever of impatient customers wanting their money quickly.

At one point George Buss leaned from his station over to Les and said, "You ever notice how some folks get downright unpleasant before a holiday?"

Les smiled. "Yes, I have noticed that, George."

But George was one of the few people Les favored with his whole attention this afternoon.

Most of the time he spent down the hallway where Byron Fuller's office stood.

Many times, when Clinton Edmonds left early for the day, Les had noticed Byron Fuller take from somewhere in his desk a piece of paper, which he always then carried over to the safe at closing time.

Byron Fuller, following his odd behavior this morning, had yet to return to the bank.

Which meant that Les might be safe in going into his office and—

"I still have five dollars coming," the blond man in the celluloid collar said. He spoke in the tone you take with a disobedient animal.

Les, whose mind had been wandering back to Byron Fuller's office, said, "Oh, I'm sorry." He could not quite bring himself, given the man's arrogance, to say, "Sir."

"You may be a wonderful pitcher," the man said, "but you're a hell of a bad bank clerk."

He said it loudly enough so that everybody around them would be sure to hear.

The frail woman with the gray hair and tiny eyeglasses standing in line at George Buss' window said, "And you're a bad sport, whoever you are." She, too, spoke loudly enough for everybody to hear.

"Don't you think he's got more on his mind than your stupid money?"

Several people laughed out loud.

The blond man, flushing, stalked out of the bank.

"You don't pay any attention to him," the frail woman said.

Les laughed. "Thanks for defending me."

She smiled. "Anytime, young man. Anytime."

This was followed by a round of everybody's praise for his pitching in general and wishing him good luck tomorrow in particular.

Around three, his lower lip still puffy and his front tooth still loose, Les had to go to the bathroom.

On the way he passed Byron Fuller's office. His heart ached with fear.

He was about to duck in there when he heard from behind him George Buss say, "I'm out of banking slips. You need some?"

Les just shook his head.

He saw that George looked at him carefully. "You all right, Les?"

"Fine."

"You look a little—chalky."

"All the excitement at the depot this afternoon, I guess."

"Maybe you'd better sit down awhile."

"Thanks, George, but I'll be fine."

After finishing up, he stood in the bathroom a few minutes, getting himself ready.

He would have to pretend to be walking past Byron Fuller's office, then duck in there very quickly and close the door so that nobody could see him.

Then he'd have to sneak back out without anybody seeing him.

He thought of Neely's reassurance that nobody would know he was involved. Neely said that he'd be sure to make great scraping marks on the face of the safe so that it would appear the robbers had had great difficulty in getting the safe open. "Nobody will suspect I had the combination," Neely had said.

But Neely didn't give a damn if Les went to prison.

Didn't give a damn at all.

He put a thumb to his loose tooth, wondering if it was actually going to drop out, and then he left the bathroom and started back down the hall.

He passed the accounting department, nodding to the women who worked there. They each wished him luck on the game.

Then he was in front of Byron Fuller's office.

Looking left, right, in back of him, in front of him.

He sweated, shook, sensed that with this act the life he'd built so carefully for himself here was about to come to an end.

But he couldn't let T.Z. die. He couldn't.

He bolted into the office, easing the door almost fully closed so that nobody could see him.

Behind his desk, Byron Fuller had a large landscape of Iowa farmland in autumn. The artist had touched silver for hoarfrost over some of the fiery-colored leaves and grasses. It was so beautiful and vivid you almost expected your breath to start pluming out and to feel the exhilarating shock of cold air in your lungs.

The rest of the office was routine, a bookcase plump with leatherbound tomes on banking and financial law; a desk that aspired to presidential dimensions (such as the vast one claimed by Clinton Edmonds) but did not quite succeed; and an oil portrait of Susan Edmonds so fetching Les was momentarily captivated by it.

But as he looked, a peculiar feeling came over him. Though he liked Susan and felt a warmth for her still, he realized in staring at the portrait that he was glad to be seeing May Tolan again. He was more comfortable with May than he'd been with Susan and not until this moment had he realized that.

Then he began his frantic search through the drawers.

At one point, he could not stop himself from smiling.

In the course of searching Byron Fuller's desk, he had found, among many other items, several sticks of licorice, a pencil drawing that depicted Clinton Edmonds as a Hydra-headed monster, and at least three different Beadle novels portraying derring-do on the frontier.

So this was how the modern executive passed his time, Les thought. But he felt no malice; indeed the frivolous nature of these things only made him like Byron more. They were similar people.

He went through all the drawers on the left, then all the drawers on the right.

Nothing.

Then he went through the center drawer.

Still nothing.

Then he heard the two women from the accounting department stop to talk right outside the door.

Would one of them notice that he had pushed the door shut?

Had one of them heard the squeak the floor had made just now as he'd eased back on his heels?

He was suspended in a terrible floating moment of dread.

He saw himself in prison—recalled all the stories friends of T.Z. and Neely had always told of what prison life was like—and saw the face of May Tolan receding, receding, lost finally in a mist, as if in a forlorn dream.

Then the two women, laughing about something, moved on and Les resumed his search.

He went through the drawers on the left again and then the drawers on the right, assuming that his nervousness had caused him to miss it first time through.

But still he had no luck.

His fingers worked through the middle drawer.

Nothing.

Then, almost instinctively, he felt on the drawer's bottom and there it was.

Taped to the rough surface of the unvarnished back side of the wood—what he'd been looking for.

He removed the tape carefully, then set about copying the formula on the paper.

He was sweating so much that drops of perspiration fell from his fingers to the paper on which he wrote, splotching the ink.

He knelt down to tape Byron's paper back in the same way it had been.

Now came the second-riskiest part of the afternoon. Now he had to leave Byron's office without being seen.

He went up to the door. Pressed his ear to it. Listened carefully.

Distantly, he heard the standard hubbub of the bank. From down the hall floated the conversation of the women in the accounting department. They were talking about their plans for the Fourth.

He gentled the door open.

Started to peek out.

Saw nothing.

He would just have to chance it. Bolt out into the hall as he'd bolted into the office.

He took several deep breaths, wiped sweat from his brow and plunged out into the corridor the way he had, as a boy, plunged into the deep, icy darkness of a swimming hole.

He stood in the middle of the hall, looking around and realizing that he had been completely successful.

Nobody had spotted him.

He felt good about himself—good about his chances of keeping May Tolan and his life in Cedar Rapids—all the way back to his teller station.

Then the gloom was on him again because waiting for him, wide and ominous in a dark suit, was Black Jake Early.

Susan noticed something different about Byron the moment he turned around.

The difference was in his eyes. The confidence she saw there. The confidence she'd been waiting to see for years.

"There's something I need to tell you," he said.

Softly, she replied, "I know about it already."

"You know?"

"Let's go for a walk."

The day was so vividly green it almost hurt to look on it. A bluebird perched comically on the branch of a pine. The air almost choked with summer.

They were ten feet down the winding brick path before she smelled an unfamiliar odor on Byron. Alcohol.

"Were you drinking when you saw Father?"

"No," he said. "After."

"That's very unlike you, Byron."

He paused and looked at her. "Are you disappointed?"

She looked right back at him. "No, just—surprised, I suppose."

"About my drinking so early in the day or saying what I said to your father?"

She smiled faintly. "Probably both."

Byron sighed. "I hurt his feelings."

"Very much."

"I—meant to."

"I know."

"He's treated us badly. No—he's treated everybody badly."

She looked at the grounds, the black iron gates at the front of the estate, the sweet smell of road apples from the recent passage of horses, the line of hazy blue hills to the east.

"I always thought I'd be happy when this day came," she said.

"Are you—angry with me?"

She shook her head. "I'm partially reponsible. I encouraged it."

"Then you're sad?"

"He won't come out of his room."

"Damn," Byron said. "Damn." He slammed his fist into his palm. "I shouldn't have handled it that way. I should have been gentler."

She touched his sleeve. "You had a lot of anger pent up in you."

"Still—"

This time she touched his cheek. "You did it for me. I know that."

"Not for you."

"No?"

"No—for us."

She nodded.

"I just wish—"

"It came out the way it had to come out, Byron."

"I feel sorry for him."

"So do I."

"Perhaps if I went to see him—"

"No," she said, "this time it's my responsibility."

"You're sure?"

"Yes."

He stared at her. "May I see you tonight?"

She wanted to smile, but she was too melancholy. "Yes, yes, I'd like that very much."

"How about Omaha?"

She said, without inflection, "I'm not sure yet, Byron."

"I had hoped—once I spoke up to your father—well, hoped that . . ."

She took his hand again, squeezed it gently. "I know, Byron. I know." She nodded to the great house behind her. It was a silly house in its way, too much gingerbreading and too many spires and too many needless rooms. "I'd better go now."

He nodded.

"I'll meet you by the gate," he said. "Save us all the embarrassment."

"No," she said. "No. Come to the front door and knock."

"You're sure?"

She watched him a moment. He no longer looked so afraid of things. "I'm sure."

Then she turned and went back to the house.

Inside, in the cool shadows of the vestibule, she paused a moment and looked up the winding staircase that led to her father's den on the second floor.

It would not be easy, she knew.

Not at all.

The second-floor hall, the maid having just finished, was brilliant with the tangy smell of furniture polish. She hesitated before the den's door, then knocked softly.

She heard a stick match flare, but that was the only sound.

Lighting his cigar, she knew.

He did not acknowledge her knock.

The second time, she rapped more sharply.

He said, "I've already told you that I want to be alone."

"It's Susan."

Even from behind the door, she could hear the sharp intake of breath.

"Go away." Anger was obvious in his voice.

"There's no use putting it off. We need to talk."

"Your boyfriend has already said more than enough."

"It needed to be said, Father."

"Then if you believe that, you and I have nothing to say to each other."

"Please open the door and let me come in. We really do need to talk."

There was silence inside, then the scrape of a chair and an old man's sigh as he rose.

He crossed the hardwood floor, the stiff soles of his shoes slapping the wood, and unlocked the door.

Unlocked it.

But he left it to her to actually put her hand on the knob and open it.

By the time she did it, he was back in his rocking chair before the window where he could look for miles across the town. Around him were hundreds of of fancy leather-bound volumes—everyone from Plutarch to Thomas Jefferson—but the books provided him no succor

or wisdom she knew, because he could scarcely read. His people had
come up from the South in a migration that took eight months to
complete, and unlike the earlier Southerners who had settled in
Cedar Rapids, his kin were not first families or rich folk, they were
instead from the poor Delta where education was as hard to come by
as a fancy carriage. He never saw them now—not his brothers or his
sisters—for they had used him too meanly, carved on his success like
a feast lost in its own consumption. Yet late one night she'd glimpsed
him staring at an old family photograph and sensed in him a great
loneliness. He would be "buried without his blood," he'd said to her
drunkenly one night. And she had not needed to ask what he'd
meant.

She went over and sat on the edge of the mahogany shelf that
stretched before the windows.

"I'm sorry it had to come out so harshly."

He looked up at her. Stunned, she realized he'd been crying.

"I'm sorry it had to come out at all," he said.

She had never seen him appear so old or exhausted. The words
seemed to come from him one by one—as if wrenched from him; and
his gaze was so vulnerable, she knew she could have pushed him over
in his chair with only a push of her finger.

He was an old man, but until now his rage and bluster had dis-
guised the fact. But there was no denying it now. He sat there white of
hair and flushed of face, liver spots browning his peasant hands, and
the loose flesh of his neck forming into wattles. He seemed incapable
of anything even remotely as formidable as rage.

She had never before realized that he was going to die—somehow
his anger would keep him immune—as if God would not dare take
him.

But now the truth had impressed itself on her and suddenly she
broke into tears and crossed to him and put her face to his.

At first, predictably, he pushed her away, but she came back and
this time he let her stay, and finally he even put his hand on her cheek,
the way he had when she was a little girl, and then he said, trying to
recapture some of the bark she was used to, "Now don't go getting
emotional on me, Susan. You're the only one in this family with a
head on her shoulders."

"Damn you," she said, but she was laughing—she had never felt giddier or sillier—but she just kept saying it over and over, "Damn you, damn you," and laughing all the time.

" 'Damn you,' " he said. "That's a nice thing to say to your father."

But he apparently understood the meaning behind it because he began to smile, as if to complement her laughter.

"I don't want him in my house ever again," he said.

"He's coming tonight."

"Not to this house."

"It's my house as much as yours."

"Did you pay for it?"

She touched his face. She was still crying and laughing. "Of course I did. Every day of my life. Putting up with you."

He started to say something, but she put up a hand.

"And you're wrong about the members of this family. My two brothers and my mother are perfectly levelheaded—it's just that you never gave them a chance. John you forced to become a lawyer and Michael you forced to become a banker. And Mother you've forced to become your slave."

"I thought you came here to make amends," he said, sounding surprised.

"No," she said, "I came here for two reasons. To tell you that I love you and—to tell you the truth."

Both of which she then proceeded to do.

CHAPTER TWENTY

"You seen your brother?" asked Black Jake Early.

"You couldn't have waited to see me after work?" Les said.

"I'm not planning to stay here any longer than I need to." He leaned toward the cage. "I've got a message for him."

A woman waited impatiently behind the massive Indian. Obviously she cared neither for people of red skin nor for people who shilly-shallied with bank clerks.

"I told you. I haven't seen my brother for some time," Les said. He talked between his teeth so that nobody but Early could hear him. "Now please get out of here."

Early leaned in even closer. "By the time the trial comes up and the Judge gets around to passing sentence, there's a good possibility your brother could have another year of life. This way—" Early mopped sweat from his face with a blue handkerchief that looked half the size of a bedsheet. "This way, if I have to take him down myself, he may be dead before midnight." He shrugged. "He's around here, Les, and I'm going to find him."

"Doesn't seem you've done too good a job so far."

Early smiled. "Not so far. But then I'm not the flashy sort. Just steady."

"Are you about through?" the woman behind Early said, leaning past the Indian so Les would be sure to see her.

Early turned around and said, "Ma'am, you've got business here but so do I, believe it or not."

He said it with enough heat that she was reduced to simpering.

Early looked back at Les. "I'd think about it if I was you. Maybe it doesn't seem like much, but it's another year you could be buying him. That's worth something anyway."

Then he turned back to the woman and said, "Now, ma'am, you can go on and conduct that almighty important business of yours."

Early doffed his hat to the lady and then promptly left the bank.

At practice later Harding said, "Well, you seen 'em, right?"

"Right," answered several of the players lined along the bench.

"And they ain't no Greek gods, are they?"

This was obviously the part of his warm-up talk where Harding hoped to persuade his players that there was nothing to fear.

"No, but they might pass until something better comes along," joked one of the men.

Several of the men laughed.

Les sat in the middle. He had suited up right after work and come directly to the stadium. He was hot and tired in his woolen uniform. When he closed his eyes, his nose filled with the clean scent of the grass that had been cut just that afternoon. When he opened them, his eyes scanned the opposing stands for sight of May Tolan. No sign of her yet.

"So don't play yourself out this afternoon," Harding was saying, "but make sure you get a good, hard practice." He nodded to Les. "I don't want you to throw no more than twenty pitches this afternoon."

Les nodded.

"So let's get going," Harding yelled, clapping his hands together, "and remember that just because they're considered the best don't mean nothing to us, right?"

"Right!" the men said.

Les only wished they sounded a little more positive and enthusiastic—and wished he felt likewise.

For the next half hour, he watched as the stands filled up with fans and well-wishers. Mothers hoisted up infants for a better look at the field, as if the infants had any idea what was going on; and daddies, being pulled, answered interminable questions from sons about various baseball teams, most notably the St. Louis Unions, who had surprised everybody this summer of 1884. Even the mayor turned out, surrounded by cronies in straw hats and carrying stogies the size of rake handles.

May Tolan was nowhere to be seen.

Whenever Les turned his attention from the stands to the field, he recognized that the team was exhibiting a bad case of nerves. Grounders rolled between the legs of a shortstop; an easy dropping fly was missed by a center fieldman who made a federal case out of supposedly being blinded by the sun; and the pitcher, Simmons, the man Les had hoped would bail the team out if Les got overwrought, was throwing one bad ball after another.

Harding paced the length of the team bleacher. Finally he said, "Go in there, Les."

Les felt a tremor pass through his body. He thought of training camp with the White Stockings.

The pressure . . .

"Did you hear me, Les?" Harding was half shouting.

Les stood up, sighed, packed a fist into his glove, then ran out onto the field.

Applause from the stand exploded.

Simmons, a redhead with blackheads, tossed him the ball. It was pussy from having been hit so many times this afternoon. "Hope you have a better time out here than I did," he said and then trotted off, head down, to the bench, carrying with him the air of a man who had just sold out his country for a few pieces of gold.

Les stood on the mound, trying to concentrate as much as possible, but still his eyes sought the stands and May Tolan.

And then he found her.

She had slipped in sometime in the last few minutes and now sat near the first team's bench.

Even from here he could see her smile.

So, finally, no longer feeling alone, he set to playing baseball.

Karney, the catcher, squatted behind the plate and held up his glove for Les to pitch into.

Karney was good. Les used his raised glove as a target. He took ten warm-up pitches and each one was a dazzler.

For the moment, images of T.Z., Neely and the White Stockings' training camp receded as Les concentrated on the first batter, a chunky man named Henning.

Les fired away. Strike one.

Henning looked almost stunned at the way the ball had come across the plate.

He eased back from the plate a little. Les had managed to intimidate him.

The second pitch was even more blinding. The umpire seemed to take particular pleasure in calling, "Strike!"

This time, Les made the mistake of letting his eyes roam the stand briefly. He paid for breaking the almost meditative state in which he pitched his best games.

The third pitch was wobbly and ill-aimed.

Karney fired the ball back with at least a small air of recrimination.

This time Les didn't glance at the stands.

Instead he poured his very being into the white ball itself, virtually becoming one with it.

The ball came across the plate so fast that Henning automatically jumped back just as the umpire, in an operatic paroxysm of bias, shouted, "Strike! Yer out!" and then proceeded to give Les a little salute.

The stands loved it.

Unfortunately, the rest of the day did not go so well.

In all, Harding let Les face six batters. There was only the one strikeout. Two of them he walked. One of them got a single. Two of them got doubles.

By the time he came back to the bench, tension had made his fingers stiff and his mind impossible to focus.

When he left the field and came back to the bench, the crowd cheering him, Harding said, "How'd you feel out there?"

Les looked straight at him. "Scared."

"You're gonna be fine tomorrow."

"You sure?"

"Sure I'm sure."

Les shook his head. "I don't know, Harding. I don't know." He shrugged. "I guess I was kind of hoping that Simmons would have a little better afternoon. In case I didn't do so well tomorrow."

Harding threw an arm around Les' shoulder. "Butterflies, that's all."

"I started out all right," Les said, recalling the White Stockings' camp, "but the more batters I faced, the more—"

"You just be quiet. Otherwise you'll talk yourself into what the wife always calls a 'funk.' You don't want to be in no funk for tomorrow." He nodded to the stands. "Why don't you go have a nice cold drink with May?"

She stood now at the fence behind the bench.

Les sighed. "I don't want to let you down, Harding."

"Will you shut up for cripes sake and just go see May."

This time, making sure, Harding guided Les over to the fence and said to May, "Take this fellow someplace and help him relax. Whatever you do, don't let him get into a funk."

"Yes, sir," May said, smiling. "No funks."

They walked along the river. In the first hint of dusk the sun was fiery gold on the water.

"It's what happened to me at training camp," Les said.

"I don't think it's good for you to talk about it. Harding's right. You need to relax."

He kissed her on the cheek. "I'm trying."

"Why don't we go have dinner?"

But by now he'd remembered Neely. "I'm afraid I can't tonight, May."

She searched his face. "It's that man, isn't it?"

He nodded.

She stopped and leaned back against a green-painted park bench that had been set along the river. Behind her, weeping willows touched the gold-red water.

"What does he want from you?"

"I—can't talk about it, May."

"I need to ask you something, Les."

"I'll answer it if I can."

"Are you in trouble?"

He didn't know what to say.

"You're trembling," she said.

"I'm fine."

Again, she said, "You're trembling." Then, "Who is he, Les?"

"Somebody I used to know."

"A friend of your brother's?"

"It's better not to talk about it."

"Is he—a criminal?"

"Please, May."

He saw how tense she'd become. "Now I'm the one who's scared, Les."

"I don't want you to be."

"I know you're in some sort of trouble."

"No," he said. "No."

"You're not going to tell me the truth?"

He shook his head. "I'm not in any trouble, May. Really."

But she was lost to him now. She had that ability. To slip away inside herself. She'd been like that when he'd told her about Susan Edmonds. Unreachable.

Then he saw Neely.

Obviously the man had been at the stadium and simply followed them along the river path.

May saw him, too.

"He's a frightening man," she said, as Neely drew closer. "You can feel his anger." Suddenly, she clutched his hand. "Why don't you walk me back to my house, Les?"

"I can't. I need to—talk to Neely."

For the first time in the two years he'd known her, she lost her air of a competent adult and became a child. "Les, you wouldn't let yourself get in any trouble, would you?"

But before he could answer, Neely had come up.

"Afternoon," he said. He smiled, but smiles to Neely were just one more expression of the ironic distance he put between himself and others.

May looked at him with the same apprehension she had earlier this afternoon. "Just who are you?" she said.

Neely's smile only broadened now. "Nobody special, ma'am."

"I'd like you to leave."

"I'm afraid I can't do that, ma'am. Les and I have some business." She looked at Les. "Please, Les, why don't you come with me now?"

Les, feeling ashamed, lowered his head.

"Our business won't take long, ma'am," Neely said in his cool, even way.

Les had not raised his head.

May left.

Neely, watching her recede along the river path, said, "She'd give you fine children."

"Where's T.Z.?"

"There's a tavern on the edge of town. He's waiting there for me."

"When are you going to do it?"

"Late tonight, early tomorrow morning." Neely's smile had returned. "I take it you got it, then."

Les sighed. "Yes, I got it."

Neely said, "Mexico's going to be good for him."

"I'm afraid for him."

"I'm going to take care of him, Les. I promised you and I'll keep my promise."

Les just shook his head and looked miserably at the ground. He thought of what Black Jake Early had said. About a year of life being better than a bullet in the heart. Was it—when your year was spent awaiting execution.

"Tell him—" Les started to say something, but then he saw the anger in Neely's eyes and felt intimidated.

You did not tell a man like Neely to convey the fact to your brother that you loved him.

On Neely's tongue words like that had a way of becoming sarcasm.

But Neely surprised him now. "He knows how you feel about him, Les; how you always felt about him. And he's grateful. Believe me, he's grateful. If there was any alternative to what we're doing—"

Then Neely raised his hands helplessly. "But there isn't, Les. There really isn't." For the first time Les could ever remember, Neely's smile looked genuine. "But we're out of your life now. Out of it completely."

Les thought of his brother living out his life so far away in the alien heat of Mexico. His only solace was that it was better than waiting for the executioner.

From his pocket Les took the copy he'd made of the combination to the safe.

Neely took it and said, "I appreciate it, Les."

"Tell him I said hello."

"I will, Les. I sure will."

"And—take care of him, Neely. I mean it."

"I know you do, Les. And I will. I really will."

With that, Neely nodded and was gone.

Les drifted over to the river's edge. Rowboats carrying lovers drifted down the Cedar. On the opposite bank a dozen fishermen waited patiently for catches. Beyond them you could see the silhouette of the business district and the first stars of night shining down.

He thought of T.Z. So much pain in his brother. And it would never go . . .

He turned and started back up the path, winding his way home.

When he reached First Avenue, a voice came from behind the shrubbery and said, "I'll walk home with you if you'd like."

It was May.

She had never looked lovelier nor could he remember a time when he'd more needed to see her.

CHAPTER TWENTY-ONE

Black Jake Early was writing a letter to his wife when a knock startled him out of his concentration.

Early had left his Missouri home two weeks ago at a point when his second-youngest child had been running a fever of 104. This whole trip the child's suffering face had stayed with him. He wanted to assure his wife that he was thinking of their little girl and praying for her and that when he got back they would, the whole family, go into St. Louis for a long weekend vacation.

He had been at the point of writing about the proposed St. Louis trip when the knock came.

The first thing he did was pick up his weapon. The second thing he did was turn down the table lamp. No sense in giving a potential killer any more light than you needed to.

He sighed and stood up. He took three steps away to the left of the hotel door and leveled his weapon and said, "State your business please."

Silence.

"I said, state your business please."

A tiny voice said, "I—" but not much more.

Black Jake went to the door and opened it so quickly it slammed back against the wall with the force of a gunshot.

He had a cowlick and freckles and suspenders and shoes so poor the toes were torn out.

He could easily have been Black Jake's own fourteen-year-old.

"What in the Lord's name are you doing in a hotel this time of night?" Black Jake said. "Don't your parents keep track of you?"

"There's just my dad," the boy said. He couldn't keep his eyes from the gun.

"What are you doing here, son? Don't you know what kind of men and women you find in hotels like these? Don't you go to church on Sunday and listen to the minister?"

"I was only playing marbles."

The kid had muttered.

"Speak up, son."

"I was only playing marbles."

"Yes, go on."

"Well, I was just playing marbles when the man came up."

"What man?"

"The man who gave me the note."

And then Black Jake Early understood. "May I see the note, son?"

The kid dug into the pockets of his frayed denims and handed it over.

"Did he give you money?"

"Yes, sir."

"How much?"

"Ten cents."

Black Jake Early dug into his pocket and put a coin in the kid's palm. "Now you've earned twenty cents."

"Thank you, sir."

"Did you get a good look at him?"

"Not real good. It's dark out."

"Could you describe him even a little bit?"

The kid then proceeded to give him a perfect portrait of T. Z. Graves.

"Where's your pa?"

"At home, sir."

"And that's where you should be, too."

"Yes, sir."

"I want you to promise me that's where you're going."

"I promise."

"And tell your father he should be ashamed of himself, letting a fine young man like you come into hotels."

"Yes, sir."

And with that the kid was gone.

Black Jake closed the door and went over to the table and set his weapon down and turned up the kerosene lamp again and read the note.

IN THE FIELD BY THE ICEHOUSE. 10:30.

Black Jake smiled.

He might have encountered more perfect setups in his time as the assistant to Judge Isaac Parker, but at the moment he couldn't recall what they might be.

Did T. Z. Graves really think Early would go to the field by the icehouse and stand around and wait for Graves to open fire?

Black Jake had maneuvered himself out of such traps many times in the past. He had a simple rule about them. Don't be ambushed; ambush.

He pulled out his Ingram.

10 P.M.

There was still time to finish his letter to his wife before he went and collected T. Z. Graves.

"You're drunk."

Susan said it with a mixture of contempt and amusement. Proper Byron had never exhibited such a fondness for alcohol before and his newfound love was both exasperating and endearing.

Byron stood in the light beneath the Edmonds' front porch. He tried to stand erect, but he weaved and bobbed a bit.

She wanted to smile but would not let herself.

"You're three hours late."

"I needed to work up my nerve."

"To see me?"

He shook his head. He had never looked more the lost little boy. "Your father."

"Oh, Byron—"

He held up a hand. "No. I insist. There are certain things I need to say."

She glanced behind her into the vast and dark house. "Are you sure, Byron?"

"Very sure."

Even though his mussed hair and wobbly manner made him seem the child, there was steel in his voice and she welcomed it.

"He's on the back porch. With Mother." She paused. "I talked to him for two hours this afternoon."

"And?"

"And—for the first time since I was eight years old, I told him I loved him. Your words—affected him, Byron. Very much."

"You're sure you don't mean devastated?"

"Yes—that, too. But they made him think. He let himself cry. I could never have imagined that happening."

He leaned against the door frame. You could see the alcohol working through his system. "But before I go in there, I have a question for you."

She said it simply. "I'm not going."

"My God—is that for sure?"

"Yes. For sure." She did her best to laugh. "Omaha has too many stockyards. The odor would ruin my clothes."

He swept her up then and held her close to him and kissed her with a frank passion that he'd never shown before.

"My God, but I love you, Susan."

"And I love you too, Byron."

Then he set her down and set about composing himself. "Now I need to see your father."

"Are you sure you wouldn't rather wait?"

"No, Susan, I've been working myself up to this. I need to do it now."

So they went through the house, over hardwood and then oriental rugs and finally over the brick of the veranda.

Mr. and Mrs. Edmonds sat at a white wicker table that the lamp glow made golden.

Mrs. Edmonds frowned when she saw Byron. But she didn't say anything.

"Father," Susan said, "Byron would like to speak with you."

Her father turned around and faced them. Oddly, instead of showing anger, he showed a certain embarrassment, as if Byron knew some terrible secret about him.

"Mother, why don't you help me make fresh tea?"

Mrs. Edmonds looked first at Byron and then at her husband. "Is that all right, Clinton?"

Clinton, saying nothing, only nodded.

You could hear birds in the sudden silence and the distant yipping of dogs and the explosions of fireworks the night before the Fourth.

Mrs. Edmonds stood up. "Byron, you had no right to take that tone with Clinton today." The harshness of her voice surprised them all. They were used to hearing her speak in soft and subservient tones. Then she surprised them all again by going up and kissing Byron on

the cheek. "But I have to say, it seems to have gotten Clinton talking
again to everybody. The way he used to."

Susan touched a fragile hand to her breast. So it had all been worth
it after all.

She knew now that her father and Byron would settle their differ-
ences.

She guided her mother into the kitchen so the two men could have
their talk.

Neely and T.Z. stood across the street, in the shadows of an alley,
watching Black Jake Early's hotel.

T.Z. made a remark on every pretty woman who passed down the
sidewalk. God knew there were plenty to gawk at. Hundreds of people milled around laughing, drinking, nuzzling each other animal-
like. The night before the Fourth was a major event.

In front of the opera house, a few blocks away, they'd seen dozens
of fancy carriages shiny beneath the streetlights, dispatching men and
woman in formal garb. And everywhere there seemed to be workingmen dressed in white shirts and blue or black trousers cinched up
with new leather belts and their women in colorful summery dresses
window-shopping or hopping from tavern to tavern or strolling along
the river and throwing pieces of bread to the ducks floating on the
warm current below. A few of the nighteries had live music, everything from piano recitals of popular songs in the more fashionable
places to the blasting joy of polkas in the Czech spots several blocks
away.

T.Z., who had still not gotten used to the idea, said, "You sure we
have to do this, Neely?"

Neely said, "You want him to follow us the rest of our lives?"

"He'd give up eventually."

"Black Jake Early?"

T.Z. sighed. "I guess you're right."

"By dawn we'll have the money and be riding."

T.Z. said, "You sure you can make it look like Les didn't have
anything to do with it?"

Neely clapped him on the back again. "I promise you, T.Z. I promise you."

Then T.Z. stiffened and pointed. "There he is."

And so it was.

At ten-fifteen exactly Black Jake Early appeared from the hotel and stood on the sidewalk smoking a cigar. For a time he was obscured by a group of passing revelers but then he reappeared, still standing there, calmly working on his stogie.

As usual, he wore a dark suit. As usual, he looked like an Indian who had had most of the Indianness worked out of him somehow.

He dropped the cigar to the sidewalk and crushed it with a big foot and then proceeded west, through the crowd.

"Let's go," Neely said.

"You sure?"

"I'm sure," Neely said. "I'm sure."

To reach the field near the icehouse, Early should have turned right at the end of the First Avenue bridge.

Instead, he kept walking straight ahead, giving Neely an indication of what the man had in mind.

T.Z. said, "Why isn't he turning?"

Patiently, as if to a child, Neely said, "He's going to ambush us."

"Are you serious?"

"Sure. He's going to sneak up on the other side of the place where I said you'd be. He thinks he's going to get the drop on you."

"So what are we going to do?"

Neely sighed. "We're going to ambush him, T.Z. We're going to ambush him."

Neely swung wide in an arc, moving along the alleys on the other side of the street, so that Early would not be able to see them walking parallel to him.

Early got up even with the icehouse and then turned right. Across the river, factories poured hot gray smoke into the night sky. There were enough small buildings and few enough lights that they lost sight of him.

"Damn," said Neely.

"Maybe it's a sign," T.Z. said.

"A sign?"

"Yeah. You ever read the astrology section in the newspaper?"

Neely's jaw muscles started working. "Don't talk for right now, all right, T.Z.?"

Obviously knowing he'd been scolded, T.Z. shut up.

This was the riskiest part, Neely knew.

Maybe Early was smart enough to know that they were following him. Maybe somewhere in the shadows ahead he was waiting for them, gun drawn.

"Come on," Neely said, and for the first time there was tension in his voice.

They had to cross First Avenue. There was plenty of light for them to be seen in. Neely had his gun in his hand, shoved just inside the flap of his suit coat pocket. Neely had never been able to get through an entire robbery without his stomach going to hell. It started going to hell now. Pain crisscrossed his abdomen. Sharp pain. He imagined that somewhere in the murk half a block away, Black Jake Early waited for them. Weapon ready. Smiling.

"Come on," he said, trying to give them both courage.

A wagon flew by, the driver drunk and singing with his girlfriend. Neely and T.Z. had to step back to avoid being struck.

Neely was tense enough that he wanted to pull his gun and waste the young farm kid with the reins. See his head burst open like a melon dropped from a height.

But then they got across the avenue and stood in the gloom. They were half a block away from the field where the rendezvous was supposed to take place. Black Jake Early was nowhere to be seen. You could smell the fishy hot river. You could smell the grasses that had begun to burn in a sun subtly tipping toward autumn. You could smell your own sweat.

"There!" whispered Neely.

Around the edge of a building that sat a hundred yards from the field stood Black Jake Early.

Neely laughed softly. "He's expecting us to come up along the river path." If that had indeed been their plan, then Early would have been in a good position to pick them off one at a time. And it was logical for a man like Early to assume that his would-be killers would indeed have chosen the small copse of oak trees to hide in.

Logical—but wrong.

Neely pushed T.Z. ahead.

They went up half a block through the alley and then cut across between two buildings. The night soaked them. Mosquitoes ripped at them.

When they reached a large warehouse, they cut along its side then came out on a board sidewalk. They went east again.

The area was mostly commercial. Small empty factories. Dark storage buildings. A dairy. Nobody worked the night before the Fourth.

Behind the dairy, abutting the field, was where they'd seen Early.

What they'd done was swing wide and come up from behind him. He'd be watching the field when they reached him—looking in the wrong direction.

Neely took his gun out.

This would all have to happen very quickly. If T.Z. even began to suspect what was really about to happen, he would bolt and run and then Neely would have to start looking for him, too. And there wouldn't be time for that. Neely expected to be on his way to Mexico by daylight.

"Ready?" Neely said.

But all T.Z. said was "I should've seen Les. Talked to him. Tried to make him feel better."

Neely spat. "I asked if you were ready."

T.Z. shaking, said, "I'm ready."

They moved.

Through patches of light, through patches of darkness. Over grass and over board sidewalk. Neely's heart was wild in his chest.

Black Jake Early was still edging out around the side of the building, watching the field when they got there.

Neely didn't wait to catch his breath. All he said was "Are you Mr. Early?"

And when Early whirled around, Neely shot him twice in the face and once in the chest.

Early hadn't had time to scream or to protest in any way. His long arms went out, fanning the air like a vaudeville comedian doing a backward pratfall, and then he dropped over with the force of a tree being felled. When the back of his head struck the ground, there was a pop and you could tell the impact had burst his head open.

All T.Z. could do was stand there, transfixed.

Which is exactly what Neely had counted on.

"He's probably got some cash," Neely said, running over to the fallen Early.

Neely dropped to a knee, jamming his hand into the man's coat pocket, pulling out an expensive leather wallet. He pulled out a thick wad of greenbacks and stuffed them into his own pocket.

He did all this without once taking his eyes off the gun that Early still had clutched in his useless hand.

Neely glanced up at T.Z.

T.Z. was still gone somewhere inside his own mind.

Sighing, readying himself, Neely reached wide over the horizon of Early's belly and yanked the gun from his hand.

Quickly, and without pause, he turned back to T.Z.

Only in that final moment did T. Z. Graves see what was really happening here.

He opened his mouth and started to protest.

Neely shot him directly in heart. He wanted him dead right away. He did not want T.Z. to suffer.

After T.Z. had fallen, Neely went over and stood above him. T.Z.'s eyelids still flickered feverishly. Neely had seen cows dying of anthrax. Their eyelids had twitched similarly. It was a measure of their agony and delirium. Nobody should have to endure that. Neely shot him twice more in the chest. Almost at once T.Z. was still. Perfectly and finally still.

"I'm sorry, T.Z.," Neely said in a flat voice. "I'm sorry."

Then he took his own weapon and put it in T.Z.'s hand, knowing exactly how it would look to the law. That T.Z. had stalked the bounty hunter and ambushed him and that in a shoot-out, one man had killed the other.

He stood up, chilled with his own sweat despite the heat. Gunshots would bring people within minutes.

He had to get out of here.

Fast.

He looked back down at T.Z.

And then felt something he never had known before: loneliness.

He ran.

CHAPTER TWENTY-TWO

Les heard about it, forty-five minutes later, when one of the boarders came back from a night of tavern-hopping downtown.

As usual on summer nights, the boarders were all down on the front porch, listening to Mr. Waterhouse.

Les was upstairs on the bed.

After leaving May, he'd come back to his home and surprised himself by falling into an immediate and deep sleep that lasted for most of four hours.

Now, coming awake, he lay staring at the ceiling, wondering what time the robbery would take place and T.Z. and Neely would start for Mexico.

He also wondered if Neely really would do his best to make it look like a real robbery and not something that Les had taken part in—

Then the words from below started to float up through the night air that smelled of sun tea and mint leaves.

"—found two bodies over by the icehouse. The police say this wanted man killed a bounty hunter, but that the bounty hunter managed to kill the wanted man, too. Say they found the man's WANTED poster in the bounty hunter's pocket. Imagine that."

"My Lord."

They met the news as human beings often do with griefs over others—with a certain glee. Misery is wonderful as long as it's somebody else's. Les had often done the same thing himself and he did not blame these people for being what they had no choice but to be—human.

He sat up urgently, as if he was about to go somewhere quickly.

But he only sat there. Muttered words resembling a prayer parted his lips. He prayed for T.Z.'s soul, thinking of T.Z.'s nightmare of screaming, "Don't close your eyes!" to their father.

So now T.Z.'s eyes were closed finally, too . . .

But his sorrow was not pure; there was some relief in it, too. There seemed to be those human beings for whom existence was a wretched and unendurable condition . . . And certainly his brother had been one of them.

Now, in the darkness, T.Z. would at last know peace.

Then the image of Neely filled his mind.

Neely.

He had killed them both, of course.

Now he would sneak into the bank, take the money, and flee to Mexico.

After murdering his best friend.

Les's moments of reflection were banished by a real agitation. His right hand began to tremble and he came fully awake now.

Neely—

For the past day, Mr. Waterhouse's story about the bank robber who had buried the bank money had stayed with him. Several times during the day, when he was not sure he wanted to turn the combination over to T.Z. or Neely, he'd started working on a plan to foil them. To take the money himself and bury it so that when they got into the bank, they would find the vault empty.

But he'd given up on the plan because, no matter how he devised it, the result would have been the same—T.Z., bereft of money, would have fallen into the hands of Black Jake Early and been hanged.

But now Les had none of those concerns.

Now he could spring his trap for Neely alone and have the law waiting there when Neely tried to sneak in.

He got up, dressed quickly and went downstairs.

On the porch, Mr. Waterhouse said, "Did you hear about the shooting?"

"Yes, yes I did," Les said.

His tone shocked everybody on the porch and a puzzled silence fell over them.

Les Graves was clearly crying.

He set off down into the darkness toward town.

Neely walked among the revelers.

He had not taken into account how many people would be wandering the streets of Cedar Rapids this night.

He stopped in at various taverns and had beers—but only carefully sipping; he needed his full brain tonight—and listened as talk of the Fourth shifted gradually to the shootings over by the icehouse.

Several times he walked past the bank. Stared at it. Twice he saw policemen caught up in the crowds nearby.

Neely would have to wait until he was sure he could get in the back door without being seen.

He found another tavern and had another beer. T.Z.'s face did not appear in his mind any oftener than once a minute . . .

Les reached the bank twenty minutes later.

He stood across the street, letting people bump into him, slap him on the back and wish him well at pitching tomorrow, and offer him declined beers—stood there making sure that he wanted to do what he seemed about to.

So many things could go wrong. He had no doubt that Neely, seeing he'd been tricked, would kill him.

But Les's memories of his brother led him finally across the street and down the alley that ran along the west side of the structure and up to the back door and—

Clinton Edmonds rolled over on his side and opened his eyes.

Sighing, he reached for the water glass on the nightstand.

As he was drinking, his wife said, "You can't sleep?"

"Oh, I got to sleep all right. It's just that I can't stay asleep."

His wife put a pleasantly warm hand on his back. "Things turned out pretty well today, don't you think? You and Susan—you and Byron—"

He shook his head, watched the way the shadows from trees chased each other across the wall, like silhouette animals frolicking. "It's not that."

"Then what?"

"I've been thinking about us taking a long vacation."

For two decades his wife had been trying to get Clinton Edmonds to do just this. To give up his tight rein on the bank, to truly turn operating control over to somebody else. But Clinton, his promises to the contrary, had never agreed. Their vacations, always short-lived as a result, were hurtling train rides to New York, where they'd stay for three days, then hurtle right back, Clinton afraid that some disaster would strike his bank in his absence.

Now he was saying they should go on a long vacation.

"Where would we go?"

"I was thinking of Europe."

She laughed. "I don't believe this."

"Susan's right. What she said about my background making me afraid of losing everything I have."

"You're a well-respected man, Clinton."

Now it was his turn to laugh. "Well respected, maybe, but not well liked exactly."

She touched him again. "You can always work on that, Clinton."

He sighed. "Yes, I suppose I can."

"Now, why don't you try to get back to sleep?"

He shook his head. "Actually, I thought I'd get up and go for a walk."

"But where, at this time of night?"

"Oh, downtown maybe."

"You're sure?"

"Yes."

"You want to go to the bank, don't you?"

He smiled and patted her hand. "I want to put some things on Byron's desk."

"What things?"

"My appointments calendar, for one thing."

"Why?"

"Because Monday, he's going to start seeing most of the people I have to now." He leaned over and kissed her on the cheek. "That way, I'll have more time to plan our vacation."

Les got the rear door of the bank open at exactly 12:01 A.M.

By 12:08 he had swung the vault door wide and taken his large leather satchel and stepped inside the big metal tomb and set to work.

CHAPTER TWENTY-THREE

Within a few blocks of his estate, Clinton Edmonds found himself caught up in a flow of humanity that was apparently determined to revel till dawn.

At first he took great Methodist exception to such a pagan spectacle. But gradually, buoyed on the floating summer laughter and oddly vulnerable aspect of the young men and women he saw, he realized that he had indeed become what Susan had said, "a proper prig."

So he began smiling and while he declined various offers of drinks from various offered jugs for sanitary reasons, he allowed himself to feel at least some small part of the celebration going on—the early fireworks bursting brilliant red-green-blue-yellow, against the silver disc of moon itself—the music of half a dozen nationalities and the dancers in native costumes in the streets.

He felt a familiar pride as he moved down Third Avenue, proud he'd played a part in this town that was becoming a by-God city.

He turned west, toward the bank.

There were greenbacks and stocks and bonds and more greenbacks in the walk-in vault.

Les yanked them from the dozens of small slots that honeycombed three walls.

He was still crying.

His loss of T.Z. rose as the shock of it wore off.

All he could think of was Neely and how Neely had betrayed his brother.

All he could think of was how Neely's face would look when he found the vault empty—

Because of his grief and his frenzy, Les did not hear the rear door of the bank swing squeakily open on its hinges, nor hear the sudden sharp rap of feet on the wooden floor, nor sense a presence in the vault doorway behind him.

Only when his name was spoken sharply—"Les!"—did he turn around.

There stood Clinton Edmonds himself. Holding a shotgun.

The man looked as if somebody had just struck him. "I—I don't believe this, Les. I—just don't believe this."

Then Les realized what Clinton Edmonds was seeing.

A trusted employee. The dead of night. The trusted employee throwing packet after packet of bank funds into a huge leather satchel.

All Les could stammer was—"There's going to be a robbery, Mr. Edmonds. All I was trying to do was get the money out of here before the robber came. I was going to get the police and—"

"I don't know about you," a deep and beery male voice said from somewhere behind Clinton Edmonds. "But that isn't the kind of tale I'd be likely to believe."

From the shadows stepped Neely.

He pulled the hammer back on his Navy Colt and then pushed the Colt hard against the temple of Clinton Edmonds.

Then Neely took Edmonds' shotgun and led the man over to a straight-backed chair. "If you move, old man, I'll kill you. Do you understand?"

Clinton Edmonds, appearing to have been completely overpowered in all ways, nodded with forlorn docility.

Neely turned back to the vault.

"You've made it easy for me," he said to Les, nodding at the large leather satchel filled with money.

"I wanted you to find the vault empty. I wanted to see your face," Les said. "You killed him, Neely. You killed T.Z."

Neely's voice lost its hardness. "It wasn't easy for me, Les, and I don't give a damn what you think otherwise. We're just animals, unfortunately, and in the end all we can think of is our own bellies and our own skin."

"You were going to take him to Mexico. Dry him out." Les's rage was becoming uncontrollable. He had never wanted to kill a man before. But now he knew he could tear Neely apart with savage satisfaction. "You were going to take care of him."

"I'm sorry, Les. I genuinely am."

All Les wanted was the slightest opportunity to fling himself at Neely. He prayed for one.

Neely turned back to Clinton Edmonds. "Get in there, old man."

But Clinton Edmonds seemed to have lost his ability to understand English. He stared uncomprehendingly at Neely.

Neely crossed over to him and hit him with the butt end of his pistol squarely on the temple.

Edmonds slumped in the chair immediately.

Neely bent to pick him up and drag him to the vault.

And Les saw his opportunity.

With an anger that literally blinded him, he hurled himself out of the vault and onto Neely.

Neely turned just in time to get a shot off, not the clean deadly shot he'd obviously wanted, but enough to tear a piece of flesh and muscle away from Les's right bicep.

Les pitched his body behind a desk as Neely continued to fire. The room smelled of gunpowder and Les's blood.

For the first time since seeing Neely, Les felt fear. Another shot ripped into the edge of the desk, splintering oak. A shot right after smashed a window behind Les's head.

Eventually, Les knew, Neely would get close enough to kill him. Les had to move. Panting like a heat-stressed animal, his hands shaking and his legs weak, he crawled along the path behind the desk to a position that put him in clear sight of the tellers' cages.

Another shot tore into the parquet flooring just to the left of the cages. Obviously, Neely was aware of what Les was trying to do. Neely fired again, wanting to frighten Les as much as possible.

All he could do was crawl back along the path behind the desk. Every move sounded throughout the quiet bank. When Les reached the opposite end of the desk, he peeked out for a glimpse of Clinton Edmonds.

What he saw startled him. Clinton Edmonds had gathered himself up enough to lunge at Neely.

Sensing the older man, Neely turned around, giving Les the chance he had wanted.

Grabbing the straight-backed chair that matched the desk, Les jumped at Neely just as the gunman turned his attention to Clinton Edmonds.

Les smashed the chair across the back of Neely's head, slamming Neely into the wall.

"Watch out!" Clinton Edmonds shouted.

Dazed as he was, Neely still had time to whirl around and begin firing again, this time with a gun he'd ripped from his belt.

As he dove back behind the desk, Les grabbed a heavy paperweight. Hiding once more, he hefted the round metal paperweight bearing a painting of the Iowa flag. He knew he would have only one chance. Neely's heavy footsteps could be heard advancing toward him, the floor creaking, Neely's cursing and breathing ragged.

Les moved. He came out from behind the desk and hurled the paperweight much as he would a fast ball. This time he wasn't aiming at home plate. He was aiming right for Neely's forehead.

Neely managed to get off two more shots before the paperweight caught him just above the right eye. This time he did not stay on his feet. He fired once more, wildly, and then fell backward into the counter running along the tellers' cages.

Les, realizing that his arm was gushing blood now, made a leap, grabbing Neely and hurling him to the floor. Several times he smashed his fist into Neely's face and then he reached down and took Neely's gun from his hand.

Les found Neely's nose with the butt of the gun and smashed it once, clean, across the bridge. The sound of bone snapping was loud as another gunshot.

Then, exhausted from his own loss of blood, Les fell to the right of Neely, unconscious.

CHAPTER TWENTY-FOUR

In the morning, they came by train and by cart and on horseback. There were farmers and merchants and schoolteachers and children and red people and white people and black people. There were even Amish in their severe black garb.

They lined the main street of Cedar Rapids on both sides. Hundreds hung out of office windows above. Red, white and blue bunting had enveloped the entire town.

The parade started way past the tracks on the east side and planned to march in the sunny, cloudless day all the way across the river. There were a dozen bands in uniforms that sported flags and plumes and hats as fancy as an Austrian guard's. The music they raised must have had the angels smiling and tapping their feet.

At noon a man in a hot-air balloon was set to perform the unthinkable—hanging from the balloon at two thousand feet from a trapeze bar.

And then there were the floats—dozens of them colored every tint and hint of the spectrum, some with patriotic themes, some recalling the days when the town had been a frontier outpost, some looking to the future when electricity and telephones would be everywhere.

One float was especially remarkable, for it recalled the Civil War, in which Iowa had lost nearly thirteen thousand young men in less than four years. The float, sponsored by a maker of baby carriages, sported a banner that read NO COLOR LINE HERE, and behind it were pushed twenty carriages filled with infants half of whom were black and half of whom were white.

All the noise and pageantry then wound back eastward to the stadium . . .

He was in and out of consciousness. The bullet in his arm had shattered bone as well as muscle and he had bled a great deal before the police had gotten him here to the hospital.

There was sunlight in his bright room with the colorful linoleum floor and the white drapes. The third time he came awake, he heard voices in the hall, one of which he recognized as Byron Fuller's and one of which as May's.

Then he slipped back into his dreams.

She came in twenty minutes later when he was just struggling back to wakefulness.

She wore a yellow dress with the vast flowered hat she cherished for special occasions. She came over to the bed and took his hand.

"Hello."

He nodded silently, dry-mouthed.

"They tell me you're going to be all right." She smiled, even though he could see she'd been crying.

He touched his right arm. It was lost beneath a bundle of bandages. "I guess I won't be all right as a pitcher."

"There are other things to be."

He laughed, a sad resonance in the sound. "So far I haven't been very good at having my dreams come true."

She said, "Maybe you've had the wrong dreams."

He looked away from her, out the window at the blue sky. "I really loved T.Z., May. I don't think he was ever happy a moment in his life."

"I wish I could have known him."

He turned back to her. "No, no, you wouldn't have understood him. I wish I could pretty him up for you but—he wasn't unlike Neely in a lot of ways."

"Neely hung himself in his cell around dawn."

And for just a moment—past his rage—came a feeling of pity for Neely.

She said, "Byron Fuller is in the corridor. He'd like to see you."

"Have the police been here?"

"There won't be any police. Byron said that he talked to Clinton Edmonds for an hour this morning and Edmonds has decided not to press any charges. As far as they're concerned, you were trying to save their money."

He smiled. "The thing is, that's just what I was trying to do. I was just afraid—"

She silenced him by leaning in and kissing him. "They don't want you to leave, Les."

"But—"

"Byron said he wanted me to tell you that, so you wouldn't be afraid when he came in."

Les let her hand touch his face. He closed his eyes. He thought of his father and brother and the ends they'd come to. He felt that perhaps he deserved no better end himself. But despite himself, his two years in Cedar Rapids had shown him that a different kind of life was possible. That there were people who could love him and that he would not always have to hate his past or himself.

Then he took May's hand and guided her gently down to his face and kissed her in a careful, reverent way that brought tears to both their eyes.

Then he said, "I guess I shouldn't keep Byron waiting anymore, should I?"

And May, touching his face again, said, "No, I guess you shouldn't."

She went and got Byron.

TROUBLE MAN

ED GORMAN

Ray Coyle used to be a gunfighter. And when he gets word his boy has been killed in a gunfight in Coopersville, he has to go there—to bring the body home. But when the old gunfighter steps off the train, he brings his gun with him, along with something else . . . trouble.

___4440-4 $4.99 US/$5.99 CAN

MATTIE

The Spur-Award-winning novel!

JUDY ALTER

Young Mattie, poor and illegitimate, is introduced to an entirely new world when she is hired to care for the daughter of an influential doctor. By sheer grit and determination, she eventually becomes a doctor herself and sets up her practice amid the soddies and farmhouses of the Nebraska she knows and loves. During the years of her practice, Mattie's life is filled with battles won and lost, challenges met and opportunities passed.

_4156-1 $3.99 US/$4.99 CAN

THE GALLOWSMAN

WILL CADE

Ben Woolard is a man ready to start over. The life he's leaving behind is filled with ghosts and pain. He lost his wife and children, and his career as a Union spy during the war still doesn't sit quite right with him, even if the man sent to the gallows by his testimony was a murderer. But now Ben's finally sobered up, moved west to Colorado, and put the past behind him. But sometimes the past just won't stay buried. And, as Ben learns when folks start telling him that the man he saw hanged is alive and in town—sometimes those ghosts come back.

___4452-8 $4.50 US/$5.50 CAN

Dorchester Publishing Co., Inc.
P.O. Box 6640
Wayne, PA 19087-8640

Please add $1.75 for shipping and handling for the first book and $.50 for each book thereafter. NY, NYC, and PA residents, please add appropriate sales tax. No cash, stamps, or C.O.D.s. All orders shipped within 6 weeks via postal service book rate. Canadian orders require $2.00 extra postage and must be paid in U.S. dollars through a U.S. banking facility.

Name_____
Address_____
City_____ State_____ Zip_____
I have enclosed $_____ in payment for the checked book(s).
Payment <u>must</u> accompany all orders. ❑ Please send a free catalog.

The Dark Brand

H. A. DeRosso

Driscoll made a mistake and he's paying for it. They stuck him in a cell—with a man condemned to hang the next morning. Driscoll learns how his cellmate robbed a bank and killed a man...and how the money was never recovered. But he never learns where the money is. After Driscoll serves his time and drifts back into town, he learns that the loot is still hidden, and that just about everyone thinks the condemned man told Driscoll where it is buried before he died. Suddenly it seems everybody wants that money—enough to kill for it.

___4412-9 $4.50 US/$5.50 CAN